Book Two of
The Siblings O'Rifcan Series

By Katharine E. Hamilton

ISBN- 10: 10: 0-692-16732-8
ISBN-13:978-0-692-16732-8

Riley

www.katharinehamilton.com

Cover Design by Kerry Prater.

Dedicated to my brother, Jared.
My Barbies lived in luxury due to your impressive
architectural skills.

Acknowledgments

It's always hard to think of everyone who's helped shape a manuscript into an actual book. I hope I remember all of you.

I sure do love my husband, Brad. He's pretty great. So here is my standard thank you to Brad. For loving me and making my heart melt.

My family is amazing. Thank you for always supporting me, no matter where my imagination takes me.

Thanks to my alpha and beta readers. Your input encourages me on long writing days.

Thanks to my editor, Lauren Hanson. We've partnered on a lot of books over the years. I'm thankful we rock it as a team.

And thanks to my readers. I love meeting you. I love hearing from you. And I love writing for you. You guys are awesome.

« CHAPTER ONE »

The view was stunning, she'd give her that much; the turbulent clouds overhead, the emerald grass swaying in the breeze causing slow waves to ripple over the lush meadows surrounding her. Heidi Rustler stared out over the vast green landscape as the cab driver removed her bags from the trunk of his vehicle. She waited patiently, the wind lightly teasing loose strands of her thick brown hair that resembled an angry lion's mane on a good day. Today, however, in an effort to tame the mass, she opted for a sloppy bun on top of her head. She was flying across the ocean after all. No need to glam up for a cramped plane ride. And cramped it was. She arched her back and gently bent her knees a bit to work out the kinks. Long legs and plane rides did not mix. And if she didn't love Rhea so much, she would have given her a big whopping 'No' to the idea of visiting Ireland. But as she stared at the quaint cottage with colorful blooms leading up its walkway, she realized she'd made the right decision. The stone structure sat a mere stone's throw away from a cliff that cut through the countryside, the sound of flowing water billowing up from below. A touch of envy flooded her as she thought of her friend waking up to the stunning view every morning. But as quickly as the feeling came, it went. She was happy for Rhea. And she was jubilant at the thought of experiencing a place such as this for herself.

The door to the cottage burst open and Rhea Conners, her best friend, flew down the stoop of stairs and jumped at Heidi, wrapping her arms around her neck in a firm squeeze. "You're here! I can't believe you're here!" She pulled back and jumped excitedly from one foot to the other all while handing money to the cab driver. "Come on, come inside." Rhea waved her forward and then stopped. "Oh, leave your bags. Claron will grab them on his way in."

"*The* Claron?" Heidi asked. "I finally get to meet the man of your dreams?"

Rhea blushed happily and sighed. "Yes. He's wrapping up afternoon milking and will be headed this way in a bit. Come on." She opened the door and led the way into a cozy kitchen and dining nook. She continued on into an open living space full of sunlight from afternoon rays casting highlights on the honey-toned wood floors. "Have a seat. Want a drink?"

"A drink would be nice." Heidi eased into the deep-cushioned leather sofa and sighed as she stretched her legs before her and crossed her ankles. "Your man has style. I like his house."

"Thanks." A deep voice flooded the room and had Heidi pulling her feet in and sitting up. Kind, green eyes sparkled as a sweaty, but attractive, man stepped into the room. "You must be Rhea's friend, Heidi?" He extended a freshly washed, calloused hand. She shook it.

"And you must be the handsome Irishman that swept her off her feet."

"I should hope so." He grinned as Rhea walked into the room and placed a kiss on his cheek before handing Heidi a glass of lemonade.

"Of course he is," Rhea added, slipping an arm around Claron's waist.

"Seeing him in person definitely confirms that moving to Ireland was the right decision for you." Heidi grinned as Claron's flushed cheeks had him slipping from Rhea's grasp.

"I'm going to shower, love." He kissed her temple. "Pleasure to meet you, lass."

"The pleasure is definitely all mine." She winked at him as he continued his embarrassed way down the hallway and disappeared.

Rhea laughed. "You didn't have to mortify him."

"What?" Heidi feigned innocence. "I can't compliment the man?"

Rhea shook her head with a smug smile. "I've missed you."

"And I you." Heidi took a sip of her lemonade. "This is incredible." She eyed the glass.

"Claron has a knack for making it."

"Now I like him even more."

"Well, once you catch your breath we will head to the B&B where we will be staying."

"You don't live here?"

Rhea shook her head. "I still live in Limerick, but I'll be staying at the B&B with you for the weekend. Then, if you want, you can stay with me in Limerick or choose to stay in Castlebrook."

"Sounds like an easy enough plan." Heidi stood. "I'm ready when you are."

Rhea glanced down the hall. "Can we wait until Claron's finished showering? He may want to join us."

Heidi's lips twitched. "I don't mind waiting for the beautiful man at all."

Rhea giggled as she wound her hands in front of her. "He's truly great, Heidi. I cannot quite believe that I can actually call him mine."

"You should believe it. You deserve all the happiness in the world, Rhea. I'm glad you seem to be finding it with him. It makes me like him. Well, that, and he's not hard on the eyes."

"Trust me, tonight at supper, you will have an eyeful of O'Rifcans."

"I'm going to hold you to it." Heidi snapped her finger and pointed at Rhea as her friend laughed. "I can picture you here. In this house."

"Yeah?"

"Yes. With Claron. You two match, Rhea."

Biting her bottom lip to suppress a smile, Rhea nodded. "I think I love him."

Heidi's brows rose. "Is that so? I could hardly tell." Her sarcasm made Rhea stifle a chuckle.

"I haven't told him yet. I mean, we've only been dating a month or so. Only known each other two months if that. I don't want to scare him off."

"Trust me, he's not scared. In fact, I can guarantee he feels somewhat the same. Though I imagine he is playing it safe like you and giving it some more time. He seems like the cautious type."

"He is."

"Well then, there you go." Heidi smiled.

At this, they heard the sound of Claron's footsteps as he shuffled down the hall, and Rhea silenced Heidi with a glance. "You smell better." Rhea kissed him sweetly on the lips as he lingered a moment longer before bending down to grab his shoes.

"Your flight went well then, Heidi?" He asked.

Heidi stared at him a moment.

"Heidi?" Rhea prodded.

Heidi blinked, "Oh, yes. The flight was fine. I apologize. I was just distracted by how much I love hearing you talk."

Rhea rubbed a hand over his damp hair as he looked up at her. "Me too," she agreed. "Wait until you hear him speak Irish."

"Oh man." Heidi held a hand to her heart. "Give me some time to find my feet first."

Claron laughed and just shook his head as he stood. "Will we be on our way now?"

Both women smiled at him as if they wished for him to keep talking and he shifted uncomfortably under the extra scrutiny. "Stop staring at me." He nudged Rhea as she wrapped her arms around his neck and laughed. "But you're so fun to look at."

"I agree." Heidi slapped him on the back as she walked towards the door. "Best grow accustomed to it, Claron. I think Rhea's rather smitten with you."

"That I am." Rhea concurred.

Resigned, but content with that fact, Claron sighed. "Why don't you two ladies just go outside and I'll be right behind you."

They did his bidding, and as he stepped out onto the front steps he held his fingers to his lips and a loud whistle pierced the air. A brown ball of fur rushed from the dairy barn up the hill towards the house, and Rugby, Claron's Irish Setter, bounded up to him with his wagging tail and his tongue sticking out in delight as he spotted Heidi. A new person for him to sniff and lick.

"This is Rugby." Claron nudged the dog with his knee to break him away from sniffing Heidi. "In the truck now, Rugby." He lowered the tailgate and Rugby hopped obediently inside.

"Your farmer is killing me, Rhea," Heidi whispered. "First, he's gorgeous. Second, he's shy towards compliments. And third, he has an adorable dog."

Beaming, Rhea turned in her seat to respond as Heidi nestled in the back seat. "I know. He just keeps getting better and better."

Claron slid into the driver's seat. "Rugby is in. You ladies buckled?"

"Yes sir," Heidi called from the backseat.

"Bang on then. Off we go." He cranked the engine and headed down streets lined with blackthorn hedges towards a small village that slowly drifted by as Heidi studied each building and each face in intense examination.

∞

Heidi hopped out of the truck as Rhea grabbed her hand and excitedly led her up the walkway to the two-story building covered in climbing roses and a welcoming red door. When Rhea opened the door, Heidi watched as her friend was dragged forcefully inside and the door was inches from slamming in her face.

"Wait!" Rhea called on a laugh. "It's not Claron out there." The door paused as a stunning man inched the door back open and sized up Heidi with a glance.

"Well, well, well..." He grinned and as one of his arms was wrapped around Rhea's waist, he extended the other towards Heidi. "And who might this beauty be?"

"This is my friend, Heidi," Rhea announced proudly.

The man kissed Heidi's hand. "Sorry for the rudeness, dear Heidi. I thought it be me little brother traipsing on Rhea's heels. I thought to steal his lass. I'm Murphy. Murphy O'Rifcan." He gently tugged her forward. "Now, if you two ladies don't mind..." He watched as Claron pulled several bags up the walkway and when he reached the bottom of the steps, Murphy closed the door in his face. "Brace yourselves." He released his hold on both women as two other brothers walked up to help block Claron's entry. The door pushed forward and hit their backs. A frustrated grunt had them laughing as Claron continued to shove against it.

"Come on now." Rhea slapped Murphy's shoulder for him to move. "He's worked hard all day. Don't bug him."

"Awe, look at that." Jace winked at Rhea. "She's sticking up for Clary."

"Tis sweet, indeed," Murphy agreed as the door knob slammed into his lower back. He hissed as he stumbled forward. "But Clary's forever cursed being the youngest brother and all. He must pay his dues to some teasing."

"Boys!" Mrs. O'Rifcan shuffled into the room carrying a cup of tea towards her chair. "Let your brother inside or I'll beat the lot of ya."

The brothers moved in sequence as the door flew open and Claron soared inside expecting resistance against his shove. He stumbled as Rhea saved him from falling forward. He found his feet and narrowed his gaze at his brothers.

"Just as fun as it was when he was a wee lad." Declan ruffled Claron's hair on his way back towards his wife, Aine.

"Not fun. Annoying." Claron shook his head as his other brothers shoved him as they passed.

"The bags," Rhea whispered to him.

"Ah. Thanks, love. Almost forgot." Claron slipped back outside to grab Heidi's bags.

"Suite two, Clary," Mrs. O'Rifcan called as she stood up once more and walked towards Heidi.

"Tis a pleasure to meet you, Heidi." She greeted shaking the newcomer's hand. "Rhea has told us all about you, and we are all so excited you've come to join us for a bit."

"Thank you."

"Sidna," Mrs. O'Rifcan added with a gleam in her eye as Murphy stepped forward and placed his hand at the small of Heidi's back.

"Come, Heidi. Let me show you to a seat. What's your drink? Wine? Whiskey? Tea?"

"Wine would be nice."

"Consider it done." He waited until she sat on the sofa and then wandered off to fetch her a glass. Claron walked back down the stairs and was immediately joined by Rhea. Linking their hands together they made their way to the sofa.

"Where's Grandpa?" Rhea asked.

"Ah," Mrs. O'Rifcan set her tea cup on the side table. "Roland and Senior are up to no good, I'm afraid."

"So they decided to go fishing?" Rhea asked with a grin.

"Aye. Though if their luck has not changed, we can't expect a feast tonight. 'Tis why I made stew."

"Better safe than sorry," Heidi added, making Sidna smile and nod approvingly in her direction.

Murphy returned and handed Heidi her wine and then sat in Roland's usual seat. "So, Heidi, love, how was your journey?" He took a sip of his own glass of wine as he waited for her to answer.

"Long," Heidi admitted. "But worth it so far. I've seen beautiful scenery, a glowing Rhea, and handsome men, so I can't quite complain."

Murphy toasted towards her on a laugh. "I like this one, Rhea. You should bring her 'round more often."

"I intend to," Rhea chimed in from her seat beside Claron. "Murphy owns the local pub. We will have to take you one night."

Heidi's brow rose in consideration.

"*One* night?" Murphy acted insulted. "The lass needs more than one night at such a fine establishment. It's only the best pub in County Clare."

"Of course it is, dear," Sidna lovingly encouraged. "But I imagine Heidi is looking for a bit of rest first. A long flight can suck the wind from your sails if you're not careful."

"That is the truth, Sidna," Heidi agreed. Her lack of formality had the family matriarch grinning in appreciation. "I plan to gorge myself on delicious food and then pass out in a comfortable bed until morning. By then I may be a functioning human being, ready to meet Riley."

"Riley?" Declan asked. "Did you have plans in Galway, Rhea?" Declan turned a curious glance on Rhea.

"No." Rhea looked to Heidi in confusion.

"Oh, I didn't tell you?" Heidi asked.

"Tell me what?" Rhea asked cautiously, not sure what her friend was up to, or whether or not Riley had orchestrated some sort of plot without her knowledge.

"I've chosen him to be my guide."

"Is that so?" Sidna, looking a bit too pleased for Rhea's taste, had Heidi nodding.

"Rhea speaks of him often. I've decided he's the perfect fit for the role."

"And does he not have a say in things?" Rhea asked.

Heidi shrugged. "Sure. But I've found me a backup just in case." She winked at Murphy and he returned it with a friendly one of his own.

Baffled, Rhea turned to Claron for help, but he only looked even more clueless than she.

"So you wish for a man you've never met to show you around and not me, hmmm?" Rhea asked.

"Not per se," Heidi began. "Just meet him and see if he's all you've made him out to be. Riley the rescuer. Sounds rather dreamy."

Sidna chortled in her seat as she took a sip of her tea. "She be a strong mind, Rhea. Best not tamper with her plans."

"I feel I should warn Riley," Rhea muttered.

"T'will be good for him, having a strongminded lass after him."

Heidi stretched her arm over the back of the sofa as Jace sat down beside her and swiped through his phone. She nosily leaned over a bit and he spotted her movement. "Not reading your message, just waiting for you to finish." She held out her hand. "Heidi."

"Jace."

"And what do you think of Rhea, Jace?" Heidi nodded towards her friend whose cheeks flushed at Heidi's boldness.

"She fits our Clary and our family just fine, I think. I also think if me younger brother messes it up then

Rhea shall just be swept away by another brother. She's the kind you keep."

"She is, isn't she?" Heidi beamed at Rhea. "Glad to hear she's won you all over. Though I miss having her close, this is her place now."

"And perhaps yours too, dear. Castlebrook has charm enough for the both of you, and I have enough sons." Sidna giggled at Heidi's unashamed smile.

"It would take more than a handsome face to convince me," Heidi admitted. "I just recently moved back to Texas and am enjoying my time with family."

"I'm so glad you finally made the move." Rhea leaned closer against Claron's side and he draped a relaxed arm behind her.

"Sort of made the move. I moved my belongings into storage, spent a few days with the parents, and then flew here. But I plan to settle more once I'm back. My folks tend to think I want to live with them." She crossed her eyes and then sighed. "Which would drive us all crazy."

"Castlebrook is pretty fantastic," Rhea continued. "Maybe once you've spent a couple weeks here with me you won't want to head back."

"Is that a challenge I hear?" Heidi asked, amused.

"Maaaaybe." Rhea grinned wickedly.

"Well, I never back down from a challenge." Heidi held up her glass and toasted towards Rhea. "Here's to Ireland."

«CHAPTER TWO»

The project was to be the death of him, he knew it. Weeks of work, multiple designs, various tenders, and nothing. The client was still in limbo, and Riley felt he was wasting his time. Heaving a sigh, he swiped his hand over the table before him and sent his drafts floating to the floor. He walked towards the windows of his temporary office and ran his hands through his hair as he gazed out over the city of Galway. He loved this city. Contemplated moving to the "City of the Tribes," multiple times, but his heart remained at home. Though Limerick was still a bit of a drive from Castlebrook, he still valued being able to take the short drive home to see his family. Working in Galway made that drive a bit longer each day, and he'd decided to stay in a hotel the last couple of nights due to long working hours drafting the layouts of his newest project. A modern art museum. The blasted project, he knew, would kill him before the end of it.

He dug his phone out of his back pocket and swiped the screen until he found the person he was looking for.

"I was hoping to hear from you." Rhea's voice carried over the line and instantly brightened his mood. The Yank from America that had stolen his younger brother's heart had claimed a piece of his and the rest of the family's as well. He counted her amongst the best, and he knew her expectations of him over the next few weeks were high. He felt he may disappoint her at the rate this current project was going.

"Rhea, darling, how's my favorite lass this morning?"

"Fantastic. I slept in my old bed at the B&B last night and was able to help Claron with the morning milking."

"I believe only a woman in love could find that task appealing." He smiled at her long sigh of contentment.

"Maybe so," Rhea admitted. "But enough about me. Why did you not come to supper last night? Heidi is here. You're supposed to meet her."

"I know, lass. And I apologize. This project be a beast. I was calling to grovel a wee bit and beg of your forgiveness. I know I missed seeing your Heidi on her first day."

"Not only you, but Layla and Chloe did as well. But you can make it up to me. You coming to Castlebrook tonight?"

"I aim to be there."

"With bells on?" she asked, her firm tone declaring that an equally firm affirmation was needed.

"The loudest, love."

She squealed a celebratory hoot and he heard the smile in her voice. "Meet us at the pub. Murphy has a mind to introduce Heidi to the best local."

"Doesn't waste time, our Murphy."

"Not at all," Rhea agreed. "See you then, Riley. Oh, and I hope your day goes better today."

"And how did you know my day was going poorly, Rhea?"

"I could tell in your voice, Riley O'Rifcan. You can't pull one over on me."

"You read me well, lass. Just a bit of a snag in the drawings."

"Then it's a perfect day for you to head to Castlebrook, have a pint with some friends, and meet one of the most beautiful women on the planet."

"Now that does sound like a marvelous time. I'll see to it then."

"Somehow, I knew you would." She laughed as she hung up and he ventured a glance at his watch. He could leave now and be in Castlebrook by the time the siblings were venturing to Murphy's pub after the family meal. He looked at the pile of papers scattered over his floor. "Meh." He shrugged, dug his keys out of his desk, and waltzed out the door.

∞

"Tis a beauty you have there, Rhea." Conor McCarthy leaned heavily onto the side of the bar as he pointed towards Heidi dancing with Gage O'Donaghue on the dance floor. Conor's presence brought an immediate smile to Rhea's face as she watched Heidi dance.

"Though for how long, we'll have to see. Once that Layla O'Rifcan gets here and sees her dancing with her lad— well, Miss Pretty might not be so pretty with a black eye, hm?" He laughed at his own joke and had Chloe leaning over Rhea and swatting his arm.

"'Tis not funny, Conor. Besides, I don't believe Layla and Gage are together anymore."

"Say no?" Conor looked dumbfounded. "I was sure that one would stick. They lasted what? Two weeks?"

"I believe it was three," Rhea chimed in, biting back her smirk as Conor tapped her glass with his.

"That must be a record for Layla." He guffawed as Murphy worked his way down the bar to them and topped off their drinks.

"She's an absolute hit, Rhea." Murphy grinned. "The lads are happy, the women jealous, and that makes for a full dance floor."

"Why is that?"

"They all be trying to outdo your Heidi."

Rhea just shook her head. "Good luck to that."

Rhea's shoulder was suddenly bumped as Layla walked up and squeezed between her and Conor. "I need a pint, brother, and make it quick." She placed her purse on the bar.

"Nice of you to finally make it," Chloe greeted.

"I was stalled by Mam. Dishes don't wash themselves." She accepted her pint greedily and downed half of it.

"Bad day?" Murphy asked, his eyes twinkling as he stifled a laugh.

"No, but you can bet it is about to be. Who's the doxie dancing with Gage? And why must she be snagging the attention of all the lads tonight?"

"Oh now, Layla," Conor began. "'Tis not right to call her a doxie when she be a new face in town and all." He motioned towards Rhea and Layla looked to her in horror.

"That be your Heidi, Rhea?" She motioned towards Heidi on the dance floor and Rhea nodded.

"That would be her."

"I see." Layla studied the woman across the room a moment longer before reaching for her glass again. "I guess I can't be too upset with her for dancing with Gage then. She doesn't know he's mine."

"Yours, is he?" Chloe asked. "And what was that yesterday when you cursed him to the moon and back again?"

Layla waved it away. "A small squabble, nothing we can't put behind us. We'll be right as rain in no time."

"Always the confident one." Murphy swiped a towel over the counter before moving along and helping other customers.

Breathless, Heidi made her way back towards the bar with Gage in tow. She beamed at Rhea and Chloe. "This man can dance." She placed a friendly pat on Gage's back and he grinned flashing a quick wink towards Conor. He then spotted Layla and his face sobered. "Layla, nice to see you out and about."

"Gage," she replied refusing to glance away from her cup.

Gage's eyes narrowed briefly before turning back to a friendly Heidi. "I thank you, Gage. For my first dance in Ireland, I would say it will be hard to beat."

"That be a challenge, lass?" Conor set his glass down with a bang and extended his meaty hand. Knowing full well the man had two left feet, Rhea encouraged Heidi with a nod.

Heidi placed her hand in his. "Show me the way, handsome." She winked at Rhea and Chloe as the stocky Conor hurried towards the dance floor to eagerly stomp the night away with Heidi.

"She's a charmer," Chloe stated. "Conor will be in love with her by the end of the night. Much like he was with you, Rhea."

"Oh, he never loved me." Rhea replied. "He just enjoyed a dance partner. You should dance with him sometime and see. Though he may step on your toes, he's one of the most fun."

"Of that, I do not doubt." Chloe admitted. "Conor always be a joy, whether a gloomy day or one full of shine. But I value my feet and shall hold onto them as long as I can."

"Aye, there's me handsome brother!" Murphy called towards the door and had the girls turning to see which O'Rifcan brother entered the pub.

Riley waved and flashed a tired smile as he made his way towards them, stopping here and there to shake hands along the way. He greeted each woman with a kiss to the cheek and then shook Gage and Murphy's hands.

"Have a plain, will you brother?" Murphy asked.

"Whiskey tonight." Riley slid to Conor's empty stool and nudged Layla's shoulder. "And why the long face tonight, sister?"

"Layla be sour that Rhea's Heidi be stealing all the male attention," Chloe baited, taking a quick sip from her straw.

Layla's eyes narrowed as she cast her sister a dark glare. "Not true."

"Ah, where is the infamous Heidi, hm? I hear I'm to meet her." Riley looked to Rhea and she pointed towards the dance floor.

"Lord of the Dance has snatched her up." Rhea watched as Riley's eyes followed her finger and settled upon Conor twirling Heidi. Her smile bloomed when she faced him again and kept pace with his quick steps. Rhea watched as Riley's brows lifted and he straightened in his seat.

"She be like an Amazon Goddess, am I right?" Murphy leaned on his elbows and watched as his brother gave the new woman a thorough once over. Murphy swatted Riley with his bar towel and Riley cleared his throat. "Right, well, she is a lovely lass indeed, Murphy. You have a smart eye."

Murphy laughed and rolled his eyes as he nudged away from the bar and headed towards a patron calling his name.

Riley spotted Gage on the other side of Chloe and was pleased to find his youngest sister's crush on his friend had faded. He knew it hurt Chloe to see Layla and Gage enjoy one another's company, but he was glad that was all it took for Chloe to see past him and perhaps onto someone else in the future. "Everything is well, Rhea?"

She leaned forward, bypassing Layla in the middle and nodded.

"Oh, for goodness sake." Layla slid from her stool and switched places with Rhea and settled back into her sour mood. Riley grimaced, and Rhea waved away Layla's behavior as if it were nothing.

"She's in a tizzy because Heidi was dancing with Gage earlier." she whispered.

"Ah." Riley looked heavenward and had Rhea giggling.

"I'm glad you made it. You look tired."

"Why thank you, lass."

"I'm sorry," Rhea rested a hand on his arm in comfort. "I didn't mean to sound rude, it's just... well, you look exhausted. You could have told me. I would have understood if you weren't able to make it."

"And disappoint my favorite American? Now, how could I possibly live with myself?" He chucked a knuckle under her chin. "Tell me, Rhea darling, where is that brother of mine you have so bewitched?"

She sighed, and a soft smile spread over her lips. "He had to check on a couple of things at the farm, but he promised to join the fun later."

"Ah, good. Clary needs a night out with his lass."

"That he does." Claron's voice snuck up behind them and he leaned down to place a welcoming and thorough kiss to Rhea's lips. She lightly gripped the front of his shirt and forced him to linger a moment longer and to steal one last kiss before motioning towards Murphy for his pint.

"Nice of you to show up, brother." Claron nodded for Riley to scoot over one stool so he could sit next to Rhea. Riley willingly complied.

"I hated to break your lass's heart. She specifically requested my presence. Jealous?" Riley raised his right brow as he took a sip of his whiskey.

"Not a bit." Claron kissed Rhea soundly on the lips. "I think she still likes me best." He winked at Rhea as he reached for the fresh glass Murphy placed in front of him. "Now where is our dear Heidi?"

"Conor." Riley, Murphy, and Rhea said in unison.

"Bless her." Claron sipped his beer, his gaze finding Heidi's as she walked back towards them. She wrapped her arms around him from behind and rested her chin on the top of his head as if they were old friends.

"About time the sexy farmer showed up." She nudged Rhea with her elbow as she sniffed the air. "Does he always smell like sunshine, Rhea?"

Rhea's face split into a wide smile. "That he does."

"I like it." Heidi squeezed Claron once more before straightening back up. Her eyes landed on Riley and she froze.

"This is Riley," Rhea introduced. "Riley, this is Heidi." Neither moved. Claron cleared his throat and had Riley hopping to his feet and extending his hand.

"Apologies, lass, for my ill manners." He lightly kissed her knuckles. "Riley O'Rifcan, at your service."

Heidi cast a quick look to Rhea before answering. "Heidi Rustler. Where have you been hiding?"

Riley flashed a quick smile before running his hand through his hair, a habit that spoke clearly to his siblings that he was nervous. "Here and there perhaps."

She squeezed his hand. "Well, how about we change that to just 'here,' and you take me around the dance floor, gorgeous?"

Speechless, Riley allowed Heidi to pull him away and left Rhea and his siblings slack-mouthed as they watched in complete surprise.

"I can't believe what I just witnessed." Chloe spun on her stool to face the rest of them. "Was our brother struck mute?"

Rhea bit back a smile as her eyes gleamed in hope. Claron pointed at her. "Don't get your hopes up, love."

She swatted his hand away. "I won't." Pausing a moment, she looked to Murphy across the bar and then to the two sisters. "But would it not be amazing if—"

"Rhea," Claron warned.

"He's right, Rhea," Conor chimed in. "Fate is best left to her own vices. Should there be a spark, she will handle it."

Defeated, but not disappointed, Rhea did a small dance on her stool making everyone laugh. Claron just shook his head, but lightly squeezed her knee.

"I don't see why our Heidi Rustler," Murphy stopped. "Rustler..." He scratched his chin. "A rustler from Texas. I like it. I don't see why our rustler from Texas can't steal our Riley's heart."

"They just met." Layla took a sulky sip of her beer and ignored Gage's hopes of reconciliation.

"Aye, 'tis true. But look at Da and Mam, theirs be the best example of a love found quickly. Who's to say it can't happen again?"

"I keep meaning to ask your mother about that. I hear it's a beautiful story." Rhea leaned on the bar and rested her chin in her hand. Murphy tapped her nose as he leaned towards her from the opposite side.

"You should. Would make her day to share her story with you, Rhea darling, especially since you've snatched her Clary for yourself."

"Enough of this." Layla stood. "I'm going home."

"You still upset the spotlight is not upon you tonight?" Chloe asked and dodged the slap to her shoulder Layla tossed her way.

"I'm not. I'm tired. 'Twas a long day."

Disbelief had Chloe shrugging as Layla gathered her purse. "Gage, you will walk me. Night to all," she said matter-of-factly and began walking to the door. Gage hurried to finish his beer and followed quickly after her.

"Do you think she even notices how she treats him?" Chloe asked the group.

"'Tis not her nature to notice, but to *be* noticed," Conor supplied, surprising everyone. A big grin split his face and his eyes sparkled as he hooted with laughter. "Didn't know I had such wisdom, did ye?"

And on that note, the mood immediately brightened once again.

∞

Riley twirled Heidi around the dance floor more than once as the night progressed, but a quick glance at his watch told him he best make his way home if he wished to be a functioning human being the next morning. Regretfully, he escorted her back to his family and friends.

"I appreciate a handsome man who knows his way around the dance floor." Heidi linked her arm with his and gently laid her head on his shoulder, and that is where she fit a little too comfortably for his liking.

She was tall, and mostly legs. *Beautiful legs*, Riley thought. And she was curvy in just about every possible and right place, making a man's heart race a wee bit faster just by looking at her. He liked how she felt in his arms, how she leaned in just close enough to taunt him with her scent before pulling away. She knew the game, and she knew it well. The give and take. The teasing and flirting. She knew how to work that incredible body of hers so that every man melted as she slinked by. Every man fell under her spell from the moment she walked into the pub, and Riley knew he was ranked amongst them. What he didn't like was that he had absolutely no control over it. She drew him in with her brilliant navy eyes and lush lips and hypnotized him with the sway of her hips like a siren calls to a sailor. Her sweet song was movement and laughter. And as he undid another button at the top of his shirt in order to breathe, he felt himself falling further under her spell. He felt smothered and feverish, temporarily void of his sense of judgment, and all he wanted was one last look of her.

He took a stumbling step away from her, his eyes wild as he held a hand to his forehead and shook his head. Rhea reached out and placed a steadying hand on his arm as she stood to leave with Claron. "You okay, Riley?"

Her concern brought attention to him, and he felt his heart race, his chest tighten, and the overbearing sense of Heidi as she swooped next to him and draped an arm around his waist. That blasted touch that had his nerves jumping out of his skin. Those maddening eyes that looked up at him with stifled amusement, as if she knew the torment she'd placed him in.

Everyone walked outside, Rhea casting glances over her shoulder as they walked up the footpath towards Sidna's B&B. The echo of heels on concrete and the early summer air tickling his face brought him a sense of calm that he needed. What was it about the woman that tied him up in knots so? He looked down at her and she winked up at him. Slowly, he felt his control come back. Slowly, he felt a shift in the game. It was his turn. She'd made her move. While he was completely unaware, she'd reached into his chest and punched his heart with her presence. Well, it was his turn now. Shock and awe... it seemed to be her style, and up until Heidi Rustler had walked into his life, it was his as well. So why stop now? Why shy away from his norm all because of a pretty face?

They reached the front steps of the B&B and Rhea opened the front door. Claron followed after her with Heidi behind. Riley stayed on the steps. "This be where I leave you all."

"You aren't coming up for a bit?" Rhea asked disappointed.

"Not tonight, lass, I'm sorry. Big project and all. If I wish to sleep in me own bed tonight, I best head home now before it's back to Galway in the morning."

"Galway?" Heidi looked to Rhea. "Isn't that where we plan to visit Aunt Grace?"

"Yes, but that's not until next weekend." Rhea added.

Heidi's lips slipped into an unintentional pout that had Riley's knees threatening to buckle. He wished to sample that pout, and it took all his self-control to shake the thought away. "Ah, well, if I don't see you before then," He reached for Heidi's hand and brought it slowly to his lips, his eyes holding hers as he kissed her palm. "You enjoy your stay in Ireland, love. I'll catch you in the city. Have a care." He dropped her hand and then turned his attention on farewells to Rhea and Claron. He felt Heidi watching him. He saw the slight tick in her throat. He felt her pulse jump when he kissed her hand. The game was on, and he quirked a grin in her direction as he headed down the footpath towards his truck. "Just let her stew, Riley, boyo, let her stew and think on that," he whispered to himself as he shifted his truck into gear and headed towards Limerick.

«CHAPTER THREE»

Heidi sat at the small kitchen table nestled in the corner of the kitchen as Mrs. O'Rifcan— Sidna, as she wished to be called— pulled another loaf of bread from the oven. The smell was heavenly and immediately made Heidi think of her own mother and how she grew up sampling, or more like stealing, a taste of the warm goodness as it rested on the counter.

"Clary brings me wonderful milk and cream," Sidna continued on as she worked. "Makes for the best butter. Here," She sliced a piece of bread and placed it on a delicate china plate with a giant slab of butter on top and brought it to Heidi. "A piece of pan for you, dear."

Heidi watched as the butter seeped into the airy pockets of the bread and made quick work of taking that first highly anticipated bite. Her eyes closed as she savored, and she moaned. "This is heavenly!"

Sidna beamed. "I know." Proudly she continued slicing the bread and placed the pieces into a towel wrapped basket. "I've had years of practice. With ten children I was forced to make bread every day in order for us to have enough in the house. The boys, oh, my boys—" She paused as a tender smile washed over her face. "They would eat four slices each, mind you." She held a hand to her chest. "That be three boys fed per loaf. And I still had three more of them! And then me girls! I'd be making four loaves a mornin' just to fill their bellies." Though she acted as if the thought were appalling, Heidi could tell Sidna missed the days of hungry mouths crowding her kitchen. It was evident in the floor to ceiling coverage of framed photos that graced the walls of the sitting room and stairway. It was also evident in the way the woman oozed happiness when her house and table were full with her family.

"I could easily eat an entire loaf of this." Heidi dipped a piece of her bread into her coffee and Sidna paused in her kneading of the next batch of dough.

"That be just what my Riley does, dips his bread like that. Teases me that it needs more flavor, though I believe he just needs to keep his hands busy. For I know it has enough flavor on its own." She grinned. "What be your reasoning?"

"I just really love coffee." Heidi shrugged and had Sidna snickering.

"Works for me." She went back to kneading. "So, what grand plans do you have with our sweet Rhea whilst you're here?"

"I'm not quite sure yet. I know she wants me to come to Limerick with her this week to check out her apartment. And then Galway this weekend. I'm looking forward to that."

"Ah, Grace is wonderful." Sidna walked over to the stovetop and withdrew the whistling kettle and poured the steaming water into an awaiting cup on the counter.

"Grace, yes, but also Riley. To be honest, I can't wait to see that gorgeous man again."

Sidna looked up at her comment and Heidi wriggled her eyebrows. "He's every bit as pretty as Rhea described him. You did good there."

Sidna laughed. "Well, you have me husband to thank for that. Riley looks more like him every day. He and Clary both."

"True. I did notice the resemblance between Senior and Clary the other night at supper." Heidi took a sip of her coffee and looked to the back door as it creaked open.

Claron stuck his head in the kitchen as he scraped his boots on the outside mat. "Morning, Mam." He walked towards his mother and kissed her cheek. He then saw Heidi. "An early bird, have we?"

"That we do, love." Sidna pointed to the tea on the counter. "That be Rhea's brew. Take it up and wake her properly."

Claron retrieved the cup. "Gladly. Sad to see you two head to Limerick today. The weekends are never long enough for my taste."

"You could just marry her and be done with it," Heidi suggested.

"Oh, now I like the thought of that." Sidna bounced excitedly as Claron flushed under both sets of eyes.

"Yes, well…" He wasn't quite sure how to respond and fidgeted a moment before stepping towards the back stairwell. "I'll just take this up." He made his escape quickly.

"It's bound to happen. Rhea has no intention of letting that man go," Heidi explained.

"Nor Clary. He was lost the moment he saw her. 'Tis only a matter of time for the both of them. Rhea suits him well.

Twill be good for him to have some company on the farm. Clary keeps to himself too much. Rhea has brought him back out of his shell."

"I'm glad she's found a home here, and a man that appreciates her. Oliver was... well, let's just say he was awful."

"You do not have to tell me, lass. He was the worst guest in the history of my B&B. But that's why I have me boys. They saw to it that Oliver was not welcome then, now, or ever."

"I would have loved to see that all go down." Heidi snickered as she took another long pull of her coffee. "I saw him one last time in Baltimore before I left. Bumped into him at a bar one night. He was already draped around some other woman." She rolled her eyes. "I'm glad Rhea is free of him. Besides, Claron is way more handsome. And *fit.*" Heidi flexed her arms as if imitating Claron's stature and Sidna giggled.

"He's a handsome lad, always has been, will always be."

Heidi sighed as she heard footsteps coming down the back stairwell and muffled giggles mixed with kisses as Rhea and Claron made their way into the kitchen. Rhea radiated love as she swooped behind the counter to kiss Sidna's cheek. "Thank you for the tea."

"Aye, and thank you for the peck." Sidna pointed to the basket of bread. "Some toast before you go, love."

Rhea snagged a slice and handed half to Claron. "I was thinking." She took a bite and paused to shift it to the side of her mouth before continuing around her mouthful. "If we head back to Limerick now, then we may catch Riley at his place before he heads back to Galway for work tomorrow."

"You had me at Riley." Heidi slapped her hand on top of the table and stood, walking her coffee mug to the sink. "I will gladly go anywhere that man is."

Rhea pointed to her friend. "See," She looked at Claron. "I told you it would not take long to convince her. You should follow us over." She slid her arm around his waist, reluctant to leave him for the week.

Claron leaned his forehead against hers and breathed Rhea in as he rubbed his hands up and down her arms. "I wish I could, love, but I have afternoon milking and we are turning over the second field today."

"I know. I just wish you could come." Rhea kissed his lips and tried not to be too disappointed.

Heidi wriggled her left ring finger at Claron behind Rhea's back as if he needed another hint. His eyes darted quickly back to Rhea. "I'll see you Friday. It will be here before you know it."

"No, I am going to Galway this weekend, remember?"

"So I have to go two weeks?" Claron's distaste had Rhea smiling and Heidi rolling her eyes heavenward as she flashed a knowing look at Sidna.

Mrs. O'Rifcan's stood pleased as a peach as she watched her youngest son.

"We will figure something out," he said. "We will not be going two weeks of not seeing each other."

"Good." Rhea kissed him again.

"Alright now, Clary, you be off. You be nothing but in the way and hindering Heidi and Rhea from their travels."

"Aye, I guess I should. Have a care, love." He kissed Rhea's palm and then nodded towards Heidi. "Keep a watchful eye, Heidi."

"Always do." She motioned her two fingers from her eyes towards Rhea.

"And you keep that one out of trouble." Claron nodded towards Heidi.

"Now that, I may not be able to promise," Rhea joked. "Heidi's a handful."

"And gladly so." Heidi chimed in as he retreated towards the door.

"That's what I'm afraid of." He laughed as he waved to his mother. "I'll be seeing you."

Rhea watched him climb into his truck before turning back towards Heidi and Sidna. "Is it just me or does he just get hotter and hotter each time I see him?"

"Alright now, Rhea, leave your love-stoned self at the stoop. We have a road trip ahead of us." Heidi lifted her bag that sat by the door.

"It's only a half hour from here."

"That's it?" Heidi asked, baffled.

"Yes. Why?"

"You and Claron acted as if you were going to be oceans apart. Seriously? It's just a half hour from here to Limerick?"

Rhea chuckled as she nudged Heidi towards the door. "Yes, now go." She tossed one last wave at Sidna as they bounded down the steps towards Rhea's car and their short drive to the city.

∞

"I'm telling you, if we take out the wall facing the gap and add French doors and floor to ceiling windows, not only will we be opening up the space, but you would have a gorgeous spot overlooking Angel's Gap." Riley grabbed his ruler and pencil, adding a quick sketch to the designs spread out on his dining table. "Yes, I know, Clary, but if you're wanting to impress the lass, at least give her something impressive to look at." Riley laughed at his own joke. "Don't be a spoil sport, brother, I'm only teasing. I think your Rhea is going to love what you have planned." His doorbell rang. "Aye, someone be at the door. Talk at ya later, brother." He hung up and walked barefooted to his front door. Opening it, he paused in surprise. "Rhea love! What are you doing here?"

"Heidi and I stopped by on our way to Limerick." She began to push past him and he intentionally blocked her path. Noting this abnormal behavior, Rhea pulled back in confusion. "What's the matter? Can't we come in?"

"Ah, yes, but... not yet." He nervously fidgeted on his feet as he saw Heidi climbing out of the car, her eyes surveying his house before falling onto him.

He felt his breath catch a moment, as her blue eyes shot daggers through his chest. A faint smile tilted the corner of her lips. "Just give me a moment to... freshen up the place."

Rhea fisted her hands on her hips. "I'm sure it's fine, Riley, you're a neat freak." She started to move forward and he blocked her again.

"Riley O'Rifcan," Rhea began. "What is wrong with you?"

"I just need to... put some things away, love. Give me two seconds." He held up his fingers before turning and darting back into his house, his door slamming in her face. He hurriedly stashed Claron's cottage remodel drafts into a sketch folder and stuffed it under a stack on his desk.

"What was that about?" Heidi asked. "Is he not up for company?"

"I have no idea." Rhea tried to peek through the window beside the door and the door opened again. Riley beamed, arms open wide. "Welcome, ladies." He backed up to allow them inside, Rhea's suspicious eyes darting over the entry way to try and spot something out of the norm.

Heidi slipped an arm around Riley's waist and squeezed before planting a kiss on his cheek. "Nice to see you again, handsome."

He swallowed as she entered his home.

"Nice place you have here." Heidi brushed her hand over the supple leather sofa as she watched Rhea hop into an equally comfortable looking chair.

"Thank you. Make yourself at home."

"I plan to." Heidi winked as she sat on the sofa.

"So to what do I owe the pleasure?" Riley asked.

Rhea shrugged. "Thought I would bring Heidi by and let her see your place on the way to Limerick."

"Ah, I see. No grand plans then?"

"Nope." Rhea grinned. "Claron had quite a bit of work to do today, so we left early."

"Ah, Clary the work horse." Riley, tongue in cheek, acted just as disappointed for her. Little did Rhea know that the work Clary was up to for the day centered around her. "And are you excited about life in the city, Heidi?" he asked.

She draped her arm over the back of the couch as she spoke. "I think so. I will be pretty bored while Rhea is at work though. You going to come keep me company?" she asked.

"Wish I could, lass. But my work has me in Galway this week."

"I was afraid you would say that." Heidi shifted on the couch and crossed her legs. *Those beautiful legs.* Riley stared a moment before forcing his gaze towards Rhea.

"Tea?" He asked.

"I'll get it." Rhea hopped to her feet and patted his shoulder as she walked towards his vast kitchen.

Heidi patted the cushion next to her. "Are you not going to sit down?"

Riley hesitated a moment before sliding into one of the free chairs.

"Are you afraid of me?" she asked.

"A wee bit, aye."

She chuckled and had him smiling in return. "Rhea's spoken extremely high of you, Riley. Seems Claron is not the only one to have captured her heart, but you and your entire family have enchanted her."

"We have a way about us."

"I can see that." She stood and held out her hand. "Come, show me your house."

He eyed her hand and cocked an eyebrow. "And why would I do that?"

"Because first of all, it's beautiful, second, I'm assuming you designed it, and I would like to see more of your work here, and third, I asked." She winked and wiggled her hand and he gripped it, pulling himself to his feet.

"Well, when you put it that way." He tossed a glance towards Rhea in the kitchen as she pulled cups for the tea that would soon be ready. "Showing Heidi the house, Rhea darling."

She glanced up and waved them on as she continued her task.

"That be the kitchen." He pointed at the obvious.

"I got that." Heidi continued to hold his hand as he led her towards a formal dining room with a large cherry stained table with bench seating. "Wow." She ran her hand over the glossy wood. "This is beautiful."

"Conor made it for me. Handy lad, that Conor."

"Yes, I'd say so." He led her to a wrought iron staircase that spiraled its way up towards the second floor. Heidi gasped as she walked into the open landing surrounded by solid glass that faced lush fields of green. The more relaxed space housed a pool table to one side and an inviting sitting area on the other, and an enormous flat screen television nestled on the only solid wall of the space. "Now this is amazing." Heidi looked up to him. "What made you think of this?"

Riley shrugged. "I like my space. Up here it feels more open. I can breathe and relax. Which is what a home is for, is it not?"

"Yes." Impressed, Heidi waved for him to continue the tour.

He walked her towards one of the guest rooms, the simple setup of bed and chest of drawers was sleek, but comfortable, as the bed housed fluffy white bedding and pillows. The stark colors contrasting beautifully with the dark wood floors.

He led her through an adjoining bathroom into another bedroom that contained two full size beds in matching spreads of white and creams like the previous room. "For the brothers, should they come to stay." Heidi continued to follow as he reached a doorway leading to his own room. He hesitated a moment. He'd never brought a woman home to his house, nor had he shown his room to one. The room was his sanctuary. It felt somewhat odd to show it to someone, especially someone he barely knew. He opened the door to the grand room and stepped inside. The king four-poster bed graced the main wall as the wall to the left mirrored the loft and had solid glass looking out over the field beyond. Sheer cream curtains hung and puddled on the floor. "This be my room." He walked towards the master bath and opened the door. The faint scent of his morning shower still lingered in the air as Heidi walked into the room. "Beautiful." Her eyes landed on the deep claw foot tub that sat overlooking the fields as well. "The entire backside of your house is glass, Riley."

"It is."

"What do you do when it storms? Aren't you nervous?"

He chuckled. "It be thick glass, lass. So, no. It's actually quite brilliant in a storm. The rain pelting against the glass has a soothing effect." He walked towards the window and looked out. He moved his hand from one end to the other. "Sometimes you can actually see the cloud wall shift across the meadow and unleash its heavy burden. Quite a sight, really."

She slid her arm around his waist and rested her head on his shoulder and studied the view as well. Riley slipped away quickly, not liking the way she seemed to comfortably fit next to him, or the way she made him jittery. She bit back a grin as if she knew the way she affected him, and that, too, bothered him. "It's a beautiful house, Riley." She walked towards the stairwell and turned at the last minute and had him bumping into her. His hand reached out to stabilize her and he immediately released her. She had an odd way of setting his nerves on fire, and he wasn't quite sure if he was ready to handle flames. *And that's what Heidi would be*, he thought. Scorching, devastating, brilliant, and catastrophic to his life. Whether for good or bad, he wasn't quite ready to find out, but his thoughts were abandoned when she lightly placed a quick peck to his lips. He took a cautious step back and she chuckled. "Sorry. I've sort of wanted to do that since I first saw you."

Unashamed, she turned and headed down the stairs towards the kitchen and to Rhea. Riley gathered himself before following.

Rhea's brow crinkled as she studied him, the extra analysis making him twitchy. Heidi sipped her tea as if she had no care in the world and as if the small kiss upstairs had meant absolutely nothing. Of course, to her it may not have. He still didn't know her well enough to know. "You okay, Riley?" Rhea asked.

Heidi pierced him with those blue eyes, a challenge sparking in them as if she waited to hear if he said anything to Rhea about the kiss.

"Fine as rain." He forced a smile and helped himself to a cup of tea.

"Heidi and I will be in Galway a little after five on Friday. We would love it if you joined us for supper. I know Aunt Grace would love to see you. I think Grandpa may even drive up to join us."

"I will think on it."

His response had her brows raising.

"Oh... well... okay." She seemed hurt and he hated himself for causing Rhea disappointment. She set her cup in the sink and rinsed it out. "I guess we better head on."

Heidi slid Rhea her empty cup.

"You're welcome to come see us if you're in town this week, Riley." Rhea set the cups on a towel to dry.

"I shall try, lass."

"I need to see at least one O'Rifcan this week." Rhea glanced towards the family portrait hanging in his entryway. She walked towards it and studied the family she'd grown to love. Briefly, she tenderly traced her fingers over Claron's smiling face. Riley draped an arm around her shoulders and squeezed. "You're completely hopeless, lass."

She held her hands to her smiling cheeks. "It's true. Odd, isn't it? That just a few short months ago I did not even know him, and now I cannot imagine my life without him."

"He's every bit as hopeless as you. Rocked his world, you did."

"Good." She grinned. "That's my plan."

"I'd say it's working." Heidi slipped her arm around Rhea's waist and laid her head on her shoulder. The familiar act calmed Riley's nerves. Perhaps it was just her way to be overly friendly and affectionate. Rhea tilted her head and the women stood temple to temple as they studied the family portrait.

"Everyone is so beautiful."

Rhea laughed and looked up at Riley. "I think so too. When this guy found me stranded on O'Brien's Bridge I thought he was one of the fairy princes I'd read so much about."

Riley's eyes widened in surprise before he laughed. "Is that so?"

"It is." Rhea flushed slightly. "Then I met Claron and realized you guys just had ridiculously great genes."

"Aye, 'tis true my mam and da are lookers." He winked at her.

"And your nanny and grandda." Rhea added.

"Aye, the nanny be a beauty, that is for certain."

Rhea kissed his cheek in farewell. "Have a good week, Riley. And get some rest. You aren't yourself." She walked towards the front door and outside.

He looked to Heidi to follow her friend but the blasted woman just stood looking at him. "I've got my eye on you, Riley O'Rifcan. Just so you know."

"That's a bit unsettling."

She chuckled. "Nothing to be worried about. I'm just letting you know now. I don't want it to take you by surprise when you fall completely in love with me."

"Is that the way of it then?" He kept his tone light, though her words wrecked him. How was he to respond to such boldness? How was he to feel knowing what she said could possibly come to pass? He already felt drawn to her more than he had any other woman. And that was terrifying and strange in and of itself.

She shrugged. "Perhaps. Will be fun to find out." She stepped outside, and he lingered at his door. She studied him once more from his head down to his bare feet. "Yes. We will most definitely find out." She winked and headed towards Rhea's awaiting vehicle, casting one last satisfied look his way.

«CHAPTER FOUR»

Limerick was a beautiful city. And while Rhea was at work, Heidi explored. She'd visited King John's castle and ate at their quaint café while admiring the beauty of the castle and the River Shannon. She'd explored the Hunt Museum and spent more than fifteen minutes staring at one particular Picasso piece before moving onward through the remaining exhibits. She'd traveled to Adare Village and explored the historic buildings with their beautiful architecture along the river Maigue. Everywhere she went, she gawked at castles and ruins, tasted exemplary food, and spoke with the friendliest people. The only disappointing factor about her days was that she had to experience it all alone.

She understood Rhea needed to work, but to say she was slightly dissatisfied would be an understatement. Ireland and its beauty were meant to be shared. She eased into a seat at a charming restaurant in Adare and waited as table staff set about quickly providing her utensils and a drink. She glanced at her watch. Eating here for a late lunch and then traveling back to downtown would give her plenty of time to reach Rhea's apartment before Rhea came home from work. She perused the menu and decided upon a mixed green salad with fresh croutons and plump tomatoes.

"Heidi?"

She looked up to find Riley standing before her, a to-go container in his hands. He smiled as he slid into the seat across from her. "Fancy meeting you here, lass."

Caught off guard by the fact that she'd bumped into one of the few people she knew and by the way his smile completely disarmed her, she took a long pull from her water. "I thought you were working in Galway this week?"

"Mostly. But today I'm in the area meeting with another potential client. Just finished a meeting actually. You be exploring Adare by your lonesome?"

"Among other things." She tried not to sound bitter about it, but the bite to her tone gave her away.

"Rhea being a busy bee, then?" Riley watched her shrug. "Come." He stood and held out his hand.

She'd eaten her salad and had been surfing her phone for a way back to downtown when he'd approached. "And where are we going?"

"You're coming with me," He stated simply and began leading her towards his truck. "Just hop in me lorry and we'll be on our way."

"Are you kidnapping me?" She eyed him with a faint grin.

"Aye, for certain."

"Well, I like the sound of that. I was just about to head back to Rhea's apartment."

He waved his hand. "You'll be coming home with me. Rhea can meet us there. I'll even try to convince Clary to meet us later as well. We'll make a dinner party of it."

Relaxing against the leather cushions, Heidi watched as Limerick flew by. "Thank you."

He reached across the console and grabbed her hand, lacing his fingers with hers. He kissed the back of her hand. "Tell me, what all have you explored the last few days?"

She went through her list and even showed him several pictures on her phone. He listened intently and smiled at her excitement.

"I had the most glorious fish and chips at this small shack by the river. An older woman named–"

"Clara?" he finished.

"Yes! You know the place?"

"Aye. One of my favorites."

"It was delicious. I ate there yesterday and promised myself I would again before I head back to Texas." She swept her hair to the side and tucked it behind her back, the long locks briefly catching a quick glimpse from him. "Everyone is so friendly here. I mean, they are in Castlebrook too, minus Layla. I'm pretty sure she hates me. But everyone else seems nice."

Riley chuckled. "Layla only be sore because there's another beauty to compete against."

"I believe she and Chloe are coming here tomorrow to stay with us."

"Sounds like a brilliant plan."

She shrugged.

"You don't seem so excited." He turned at a stoplight and began heading East towards the outskirts of Limerick and towards his house.

"It's not that. I've just barely had any time with Rhea since I've been here."

"Perhaps tonight we can change that, hmm?"

"Maybe. Though if Claron is there, I'm not sure." Her tone held warmth, though he could see she was still disappointed. "I sound like I'm whining, and I don't mean to be. It's just... I came to see her, and I haven't really gotten to do that."

"Her loss is my gain." Riley winked at her as he eased to a stop outside his beautiful house. "Come. We'll have a wee tipple before everyone else arrives."

"I have no idea what that means, but it sounds fun, so I'm going to say yes."

He laughed as he unlocked his front door and keyed in his alarm code. "A drink, lass. Only a drink." He led the way to his kitchen and grabbed a fresh bottle of wine, making quick work of opening it and letting it breathe on the counter.

"So what is this project you're working on in Galway?" She asked, sliding onto a stool at the bar.

"An art museum. Though me client can't settle upon a final layout, I may be moving on. Sort of turning into a time suck at the moment, and I'm not one to like being idle."

"I've visited a few museums this week. My favorites were the ones that were more cozy than open. The ones with white walls and stark lighting give me a headache."

He listened and took a test sip of the wine in his glass before pouring. "That so?"

"I know lighting is important, but the ambiance of a smaller, welcoming space was more exciting."

"Noted."

"I'm sorry." She shook her head and took a long sip of the dry red wine. "You're the architect and the expert."

"True." He grinned when she looked up. "But I also value input, especially from someone who would be visiting the premises."

"I doubt I will. Won't be finished before I leave, I'm sure."

"If you leave," he added.

"Oh, do you plan on making me stay?" She leaned forward on the bar and stared him straight in the eyes. He took a nervous step back and sipped from his glass, watching as uncertainty washed over her.

"Rhea did."

"I'm not Rhea."

"That is for certain."

"What's that supposed to mean?" she asked, her hackles rising.

He held up his hand. "I did not say it was a bad thing, lass. In fact, I happen to like that you're different than our Rhea. I love Rhea," he amended. "But 'tis nice to meet a lass like you as well."

"Good reply."

He laughed, the sound deep and pleasing. She tapped her glass to his. "How about I beat you at pool?" She pointed towards the ceiling.

"That be a challenge, lass?"

"I love challenges."

Her attitude shifted from annoyance to flirtation and she swung her feet to the floor and began leading the way upstairs as if she owned the place. Riley followed, carrying the rest of the bottle with him. "Prepare yourself, Riley O'Rifcan, for I am quite good." She began chalking her stick and his eyes sparked.

"Aye, that you are," he whispered, setting his glass aside and grabbing his own stick. When she handed him the chalk, he gripped her hand a moment and met her gaze. Her stomach flipped at the look in his eyes, but he slowly eased away and acted as if nothing had just happened. Racking the balls on the table, she watched as he set the white ball on the green felt. "Ladies first, love."

∞

Riley laughed as Heidi attempted a trick shot, the stick behind her back as she aimed towards a striped ball and called corner pocket. When it went in, she released a celebratory hoot and walked around the table to survey her next shot. She was better than he expected. In fact, she was currently beating him, but he didn't care because at the moment he could not think of anything better than watching Heidi play pool. She was too glorious a sight to not enjoy and as his phone buzzed in his pocket, he regretfully took his eyes away from her for one moment as he read his text.

As he started to respond, Heidi yanked his phone from his hand. "Your turn." She set the phone aside as Riley circled the table. "Hope it wasn't urgent." She grimaced, and he shook his head.

"Just a lass." He made his shot and glanced up. "Jealous?"

She tossed her hair over her shoulder as she passed him. "Never." She took her place and nudged him with her hip. "Excuse me, you're in my way." She leaned over to set up her aim and felt him staring at her.

"Guess I will tell her I'm free tomorrow night, then." Riley bit back a smile as he saw her shoulders stiffen as he lazily walked back towards his phone.

"Is she in Galway?"

"Maybe. Maybe not." He ran his fingers over his phone in quick response.

"Well, isn't that where you will be tomorrow? For work?"

"Tomorrow, yes. Tomorrow night..." He shrugged. "That's what I'm trying to plan, is it not?"

She squinted as if trying to read him. When he finished his text, he caught the brief look of disdain and grinned.

"Your turn." She took a long sip of her wine as she watched him.

"So tell me, Heidi," He circled behind her and liked that he was now making her nervous and not the other way around. "There be a lad waiting for you in Texas?"

"No. Why?"

"Just curious." He winked at her as he leaned forward to line up his shot.

"Would I have kissed you the other day if I had a man?"

He shrugged. "I don't know. I don't know you well enough. You could be a lass who kisses any man she likes."

"Well, I'm not." She fisted her free hand on her hip as she rested against her stick.

He liked that her tone held offense.

"And do you have a woman, Riley? Since we are on the subject and one seems to be texting you."

He smirked. "Not one in particular, no."

"So you have many?"

"That'd be a no as well. I have friends. That are female. That I enjoy sharing a dinner with now and again."

"I see." She watched as he missed his shot and his phone buzzed again. A cheeky grin spread over his face as he responded. "Okay." she walked over to him and slipped his phone from his hand.

Intrigued, he let her set it aside again. "I don't mind who you eat with tomorrow night, but tonight you're with me, so she can wait." She walked back towards the pool table and made her shot, successfully narrowing down her ball count to just the solid black ball sitting in the farthest corner from her.

"Apologies if I was rude, lass."

"Not rude. Annoying." She blew her bangs out of her eyes and pointed her stick to the pocket diagonal from her. "Left corner pocket." She leaned down and aimed, missing by a hair. She hissed in disappointment.

"Annoying, how?"

She looked at him, her navy eyes sharp. "When I'm with someone, whether as a friend or more, I try not to be on my telephone. They're the one I'm spending time with and therefore receive my focus. I expect the same treatment in return."

Feeling rather scolded, but also impressed, Riley walked towards her and fetched her hand in his. He kissed her knuckles. "It won't happen again."

His phone buzzed and he ignored it by walking around the table to make his next shot. "For what it's worth, it be Rhea's Aunt Grace."

He watched as her face blanched and he laughed. "She be hounding me about meeting her for dinner when you two are in Galway."

"Oh." Heidi blushed and ran an embarrassed hand over her face.

He grabbed her hand and pulled it to her side. "Don't be embarrassed, love. I like that you feel a wee bit of envy."

She swatted him, and he ducked away as he continued laughing.

"I'm not jealous. I just find it aggravating."

"Mmhmm." He acted like he didn't believe her and could see her annoyance growing. The doorbell rang, and he held up a finger. "Peace offering? We have guests."

She huffed passed him and set her stick against the wall. Riley, still amused, chuckled as she shot daggers at him with her eyes on her way down the stairs. "Best hurry it up, O'Rifcan. I'm answering your front door!"

Shaking his head and feeling mighty pleased, Riley followed her down.

∞

"Claron!" Heidi opened the door and jumped into the man's arms. Surprise flickered over his face as he looked to see his brother coming down the stairs.

"Heidi," Claron greeted as she pulled back.

"I'm so glad you're finally here. Your brother is a complete nuisance."

"Aye, I've heard that one before." He shook Riley's hand as Heidi continued to drag him through the house by the other.

"We have wine upstairs where I was beating Riley at pool."

"Beating him, were you?"

"Indeed." Riley nodded towards Heidi. "She's impressive, brother. You should see her."

"Rhea not here yet?" Claron asked.

"No. Come to think of it, I'm not sure if I told your Rhea of our plans." Riley scratched his head in thought. "I don't believe I did. Best call her, Clary. I would, but Heidi gets nasty jealous when me attentions are on another woman." A slap hit him upside the head as she walked by him towards Claron, extending a glass of wine.

"I texted her earlier, Claron. She'll be here." Heidi watched with a pleased smirk as Riley rubbed the back of his dark locks.

Claron eased onto the sofa. "'Tis a good wine, Riley. Much needed after today."

"Did you get your ladies taken care of?" Riley asked, as he sat in one of the free chairs, Heidi not far behind him. She sat on the arm rest of his chair and felt a small glint of satisfaction when she saw his eyes dart to her legs.

"Aye. Murphy helped me wrap it up today, so I could make it."

"Rhea will be pleased."

A tender smile spread over Claron's face. "I'm hoping so." He turned his attention to Heidi. "And how's your week in Limerick been?"

"Good. Been seeing the sights. Ready to spend some time with Rhea this weekend though."

"You're welcome to come to Castlebrook any time, if Rhea's busy. I know Chloe and Layla would enjoy showing you around."

"I was thinking more of Murphy showing me around Castlebrook," Heidi admitted. "I believe I'm still blacklisted where Layla is concerned."

"She's been in a tizzy, hasn't she?" Claron agreed. "This Gage business best wrap up soon or I feel we all may feel her wrath."

"Did we not call this?" Riley asked in annoyance. "We knew it would end in flame. It's Layla's way. No friend of ours is safe, Clary, once Layla's turned a glad eye on them."

"As if the man does not have a choice," Heidi scoffed.

"Not with Layla," both brothers muttered.

"So she goes after what she wants. That's a good thing."

"Not when it always be our friends," Riley pointed out. "Every. Single. Time. And then it changes things amongst our mates. 'Tis hard being friends after your sister breaks their hearts."

"And have you dated any of her friends?"

"That would be a no," Riley proudly stated.

"And you?" She pointed to Claron and he shook his head.

"Any of the other brothers?"

"I believe Murphy flattered one or two here and there, but nothing serious," Riley stated. "But he still be friends with them and they friends with Layla. Murphy keeps friends easily, Layla does not."

"She just wants to find a good lad," Claron defended half-heartedly and Heidi smiled at his effort.

A knock sounded at the front door and Claron hopped to his feet. "That be Rhea, I'm guessing. I'll welcome her."

"Welcome her properly, Clary, but no snogging in the front entry."

"No promises." Claron playfully punched his brother's shoulder as he headed towards the door. They could hear Rhea greet him with a kiss and then inquire about the other two.

"I like him," Heidi said. "Every time I'm near him, he makes me smile."

"Clary be a great lad. Always has been. A steady one is our Clary. No one more dependable."

"I like you too," she admitted openly. "So when are we going to do something about that?"

"And what do you wish for me to do about that?"

"Do you not like me too?"

"Find you attractive, yes. Find you decent company, yes. But do I care for you? No. Not yet. I don't know you well enough for that."

"That's fair." Heidi, unoffended, slid into her own chair. "Perhaps you could get to know me."

"Perhaps I might during your stay." Riley stood to greet Rhea with a hug.

"And how are two of my favorite people?" She gave Heidi a hug as well.

"Oh, I was just trying to convince Riley to ask me out." Heidi grinned as Riley just shook his head in bewilderment.

Rhea laughed. "And how is that going?"

"He's playing hard to get."

Riley held up his hands as if he couldn't help it and Rhea winked at him. "Keep trying. I think you're beginning to wear him down."

"I think so too." Heidi smirked at Riley. "So, what are we doing for dinner, Mr. O'Rifcan?"

Riley's brows rose as he walked towards the kitchen. "Let me see what I have in my cupboards. Clary, you can assist me. Ladies, you settle at the bar with your drinks and keep us company."

"Now that is an offer I can't refuse." Rhea slid onto a bar stool and heaved a tired sigh, Claron kissing the top of her hair as he passed by.

Heidi patted her friend's back. "How was work?"

"Good. More training today. Delaney has about had enough of me shadowing him, I think."

"Delaney?" Heidi asked.

"My boss." Rhea took a sip of her wine. "I mean, he's great, it's just a lot to take in. Things are done a bit differently here than in the U.S., not to mention a different currency all together. So just some adjusting."

"You'll catch on," Claron encouraged.

"Swimmingly," Riley agreed.

Rhea softened. "Thanks, guys. I know I will. Just feeling a bit overwhelmed lately. *But* enough about me. How was Adare today?" She slapped Heidi's thigh.

"Beautiful. As you promised. Though I will admit I was starting to tire out when Riley found me."

"What were you doing in Adare?" Rhea asked.

Riley eyed Claron briefly and his brother ignored him. "A new project."

"Ah. That would be a neat area to work."

"I wouldn't be working there. Just looking for specific materials there."

"I see. What materials?" Rhea asked.

Riley cleared his throat for Claron to help explain, but his brother remained completely silent. Heidi picked up on Riley's silent cues and curiously furrowed her brow. "Just some certain building materials that are exclusive to the area. Pretty tiles and such."

"Neat." Satisfied, Rhea went about stealing a piece of cheese that Claron had cut.

Heidi waited until Riley looked her way and he gave a quick shake of his head for her not to ask further questions. She complied, knowing full well the brothers held a secret between them that they did not wish for Rhea to find out.

«CHAPTER FIVE»

Riley swirled the whiskey in his glass as he sat staring out over the meadow. His house was quiet now that everyone had left for home; Rhea and Heidi towards Limerick, Clary towards Castlebrook, and he just sitting, sipping whiskey alone. He normally liked the quiet house. But ever since having Heidi here, all he could think of was how much he liked her presence. She was bold, he'd give her that. Still wasn't quite sure how he felt about her open pursuit of him, but at the same time, she intrigued him.

Sighing, he stood and trudged towards his bedroom. The last thing he wanted was to tangle with one of Rhea's friends, especially one on holiday. He knew that should he invest time into

Heidi, he most definitely would not want her traveling back to Texas. Something about her had his heart wavering. He'd purposely refrained from any serious relationships the last several years so as not mess up the path he was on professionally. He wanted to excel in his architecture practice, and he couldn't do that if he was distracted. And Heidi would be more than a distraction. She wasn't the type of woman a man dated for a quick fling of fun. She was the type of woman to wrap around his heart and demand a lifetime from him. Riley was not ready for a lifetime commitment. But there was also something special about Heidi that he'd be a fool not to notice. No woman had ever captivated or confused him the way she did.

Brooding into the mirror wasn't his style, but yet, there he was, staring into the bathroom mirror pondering over a blasted woman he'd known all of a week. Disgusted with himself, he made quick work of turning on the shower.

He appreciated good design. He watched as the water puddled around his feet. It was one of the reasons he designed his own home, down to the very knobs in his shower. And appreciating good design meant he appreciated Heidi. She was a work of art. He groaned, and there he was, thinking of her again. What spell did she have him under? What faeries had fogged his brain? He turned the hot water to freezing cold and gasped as it pelted his back. There. Shock her out of his system. Turning off the water, he stepped out of the shower and donned his favorite sweats. He'd just settle in for a night of working on Claron's house plans. Working on a project for his brother and Rhea would help rid him of the bewitching thoughts of Heidi.

His phone buzzed and a number he didn't recognize popped up on his text messages.

"Dinner was fabulous, handsome. Thanks for rescuing me today."

Feeling grim, he tossed the phone on his desk as he retrieved Claron's sketches. How was he to stop thinking of her when she kept popping up?

Reluctantly, he reached for his phone.

Riley: *No problem, lass. Glad you came.*

Heidi: *Will I see you Friday in Galway?*

Riley: *Planning on it.*

Heidi: *Good. I like the look of you, Riley O'Rifcan. Can't wait to see you then.*

"Blast!" Riley dropped the phone again and rubbed his hands through his wet hair trying to think of a response.

Riley: *Have a care, lass.*

There. He kept it simple and cordial. In no way encouraging. Another message dinged.

Rhea: *Thanks for dinner, Riley. You're the best for hanging out with Heidi today. I know she's been a bit bored, and it means a lot that you showed her around a bit. I owe you one.*

Riley: *You owe me nothing, love. 'Twas my pleasure.*

Rhea: *You're sweet. I must warn you, she's talked about you nonstop.*

A smiley face with heart eyes appeared on the screen.

He wasn't quite sure how to respond.

Rhea: *I know she may come on a bit strong, but she truly is a great person. There. I did my part. I will not try to convince you of her greatness beyond this point.*

He snickered, knowing full well that if Rhea had it in her mind to matchmake all she'd need to do is put his mother onto it and her work would be fulfilled by someone else. He supposed he should be flattered that Rhea found him good enough for her best friend. That thought warmed him, but again, Heidi was dangerous. Dangerous to his way of life. And he liked his life the way it was. Or did, before she showed up. Time would tell. Perhaps Galway would be a good time to survey her again.

He wanted to know her better. To know what she loved, hated, what scared her? Did anything scare a woman like that? He doubted it. But he wanted to know more intimate details before diving in head first. Caution was new to him. Typically, he didn't mind a nice dabble of fun here and there. He'd broken a few hearts in his days. But Heidi's was not a heart he wished to break, and in so doing break Rhea's. He'd never forgive himself. Caution was necessary. The situation needed to be handled delicately. He could do it. And should he feel himself falter, he'd just leave. He was busy. He had good excuses. Yes, that's what he'd do. Galway was his city. He'd show her a good time, and when things grew too much for him, he'd bolt. That didn't make him a coward, just cautious. Right?

He rubbed a hand over his face as he headed back upstairs and flopped onto his bed and covered his head with his pillow. He just needed to sleep on it all. Maybe then he'd feel better about it. Hopefully.

∞

"So, plans changed." Rhea tossed a pillow at a still sleeping Heidi and waited. Heidi eased to her elbows peeping over the side of the couch and swiped her hair from her eyes.

"What?" she mumbled.

"Our plans to head to Galway for the weekend have changed. Aunt Grace received an offer she couldn't refuse, apparently." Rhea rolled her eyes.

"Meaning a man."

"Yep. A man and a trip to Fiji."

"Must be nice."

"Right?" Rhea tossed her cell phone onto the kitchen bar. "I'm kind of bummed, but also excited that we can just head to Castlebrook anyway."

Heidi snuggled her face back into her pillow.

"Don't fall back asleep. Let's get moving. The sooner we leave the more time we have there." Rhea walked over and ripped back the blanket covering Heidi's legs.

Heidi groaned. "Don't take this the wrong way, but I really hate you right now."

Rhea grinned. "Hate me all you want, at least you will have a warm shower. I could have used all the hot water."

"You wouldn't dare." Heidi stood and stretched as she slowly trudged down the hallway towards the bath.

"Be sure to wear something pretty, I'm sure we'll see Riley today," Rhea taunted.

Heidi turned with a smirk. "Noted."

It never really took her long to get ready. She wasn't one for wearing gobs of makeup, and she wasn't the type of girl to stand in front of the mirror and change her outfit multiple times. You got what you saw with her. Take it or leave it. And as she donned a pair of white shorts and a pale blue off the shoulder top, she felt comfortable and relaxed. The shorts showcased her long legs and her tan, and the shirt showcased her shoulders. What else did she need? She shrugged and fluffed her hair with her fingers, the wild mass falling in natural waves well past her shoulders.

"You look gorgeous." Rhea leaned on the door jam to slip a sandal on her foot. "Ready?"

"As I'll ever be."

"Great." Rhea smiled as she walked towards the front door and grabbed her keys and a small duffle bag.

Heidi wheeled her suitcase down the hall.

"Why are you taking your suitcase? I left you a small bag to use for the weekend."

"Rhea," Heidi paused a moment, hoping not to hurt her friend's feelings. "I love you, and I've loved seeing Limerick. But I think I'm going to stay in Castlebrook this week instead."

"Oh."

"Are you mad?"

"No." Rhea sighed. "I know it wasn't ideal for me to work the whole time you were here. At least in Castlebrook you'll have Chloe and Layla to hang out with."

Heidi pointed at her as if she hit the nail on the head.

"I'll just drive up a couple evenings after work and have the meal with the family."

"See, all works out. And you'll get to see your gorgeous farmer."

"That's always a bonus." Rhea walked out the door and waited for Heidi to clear the threshold before locking it behind them. "I texted Chloe earlier. We're going to meet at McCarthy's Restaurant for lunch with her and Layla. Afterwards, if we feel like it, we'll either go to the pub or hang out at Layla's place."

"Either sounds fine with me." Heidi slipped into the car and glanced at her phone as Rhea pulled out into city traffic. Thankful the drive wasn't a long one, and that food would be at the other end of it, she focused on her text messages with Riley from the night before. "So, tell me more about Riley."

Rhea's brows rose. "What do you want to know?"

Heidi shrugged. "Anything. You made him sound like a flirt, but he's barely flirted with me since I've been here, and trust me, I've been bringing my A game."

Laughing, Rhea shook her head. "Maybe you scare him."

"He did admit to that. I thought he was kidding. But maybe I have scared him off. Which is a real shame, because he is... nice."

"Nice?" Rhea giggled.

"Of all things that was the best description I could think of."

"Riley's great. He's been my saving grace multiple times since moving here. He rescued me my first day, he always cheered me up when Oliver would hound me. He helped rid my life of Oliver, and he's basically turned into one of my best friends. He's an amazing guy. He is flirty, usually," she added. "But he's respectful. He's not a player by any means, he just appreciates making women feel good about themselves. If he's interested in a woman, he makes the moves. That might be why you've scared him so much. You're a go-getter. He's not used to that. He's used to it being the other way around. You've thrown him off his game."

"I should have just kept my mouth shut the other night."

"What did you say the other night?"

"Oh lots of things. All of which I'm sure makes him think I have terrible intentions."

Rhea frowned. "I'm sure he doesn't think that. Like I said, he's just not used to being the one pursued. Flirted with, yes. Pursued, no. He's usually the pursuer."

"So I should back off?"

Rhea shrugged. "Why do you want his attention in the first place? What is it about him that has you so interested?"

"You would think I'm crazy," Heidi replied dismissively.

"I doubt you could be any crazier than I already think you are," Rhea teased and was rewarded with a faint smile.

"Okay." Heidi inhaled a deep breath. "There's just something about him. When I saw him at the pub for the first time, it was like all the air in the room, and my lungs, was just sucked away. Everything was still. And my heart jumped in my chest and my fingers tingled. *Literally* tingled."

Rhea giggled.

"And when he talks to me... I seriously could listen to him talk *all* day. His voice sends my stomach dancing. When we played pool last night, his presence was overwhelmingly intoxicating. And it's like he doesn't even try to be like that. He just is."

"I think the same thing about Claron. Those O'Rifcan brothers sure know how to twist a girl up inside, don't they?"

"I've never been like this," Heidi admitted. "Not even with Chase. And I was with him for three years!" Exasperated, Heidi ran her hands through her hair. "I mean, you call and tell me how great this Riley man is... okay, sure. Sounds great. But then I see him and bam! It's like everything you've said about him just hits me in that moment and I'm faced with the real thing. The real-life, breathing, handsome package that exudes a confidence and caring attitude towards you and everyone else he interacts with and I can't help myself. I'm a goner."

Rhea pulled silently into Castlebrook and towards the restaurant owned by Conor's family. The windows boasted McCarthy's Restaurant in bold white letters and a green canopy draped over the entrance. Rhea parked in front.

"But I've scared him off. I'm sure of it," Heidi continued. "He probably thinks I'm crazy." She shook her head as she unbuckled and stepped out. A silver truck pulled into the parking lot next to her as she shut her door, barely missing clipping it. "Sheesh!" She jumped a bit as a broad smile of the driver flashed at her. "What is he doing here?" She asked.

Riley hopped out of his truck and swooped towards Heidi and kissed her cheek. "Greetings love, best be on your toes." He then pulled Rhea towards him and kissed her cheek as well.

Heidi's heart pounded in her chest. He was more relaxed than he was the night before. Friendlier. And he kissed her cheek. His eyes roamed over her as he held out his arm. "Shall I make all the lads jealous by escorting two beautiful women inside?"

Rhea and Heidi both linked their arms with his.

"Only this once," Claron called from behind him as he trotted to catch up having parked around the corner. He opened and held the door for them as Riley squeezed through with both women on his arms.

Conor poked his head from behind the kitchen door and beamed at his friends. "Best call the coppers, Mammy!" He yelled over his shoulder. "The O'Rifcan brothers are here to cause a rumpus!" His booming laugh echoed about the room as he laughed at his own joke and pointed to a long table where Chloe and Layla awaited them.

Chloe smiled in welcome and patted the seat next to her for Heidi. "Tell me of your Limerick adventures."

Rhea and Claron sat opposite them, and Riley on the other side of Heidi. Layla sat at the head of the table studying Heidi.

"It was great." Heidi reached for the water Conor placed in front of her and took a sip. "Everywhere you go in this country it's beautiful. I really enjoyed the art museums and all the great food along the way."

"Limerick does have some delicious spots." Chloe agreed. "Though nothing beats our Mam's and Mrs. McCarthy's cooking." She nodded towards Conor as he continued placing drinks around the table. He acknowledged her with a grateful nod in return.

"I can agree with that. I'm still dreaming about your mother's bread."

Chloe giggled. "She has a knack for it, that's for certain. 'Tis why Lorena, Layla, and I have never been skin and bones."

"I look forward to gorging myself on it all this week."

"You be staying in Castlebrook then?" Chloe asked.

"She is," Rhea interrupted. "I bored her to death in Limerick."

"Not true." Heidi rolled her eyes at Rhea. "Just want to see more of Castlebrook."

"Well perfect timing then. We be getting ready for the flower festival. If you wish for something to do, I could use some help at me shop."

"Sure. What kind of shop?"

Riley leaned towards her. "Our Chloe be the town florist."

"Oh," Heidi thought it over. "This is a busy week for you then. I would love to help you. Though I don't know much about flowers."

"Our Chloe be the best teacher." Conor tucked his tray under his arm as he waited to take orders. "Gifted by the fairies she was. Touches a petal and it blooms to perfection."

Chloe flushed at the praise and Riley reached behind and around Heidi to squeeze his sister's shoulder. "That be the truth of it," he agreed.

"Then it sounds like an opportunity that can't be beat." Heidi beamed at Rhea across the table.

"Except maybe an evenin' at the pub dancing the night away with me, of course." Conor winked at her as he looked to Layla. "What be your fancy, lass?"

Layla ordered a salad and Conor worked his way around the table. Rhea ordered a large pizza and had everyone staring at her in surprise. She laughed. "I'm ordering so I have leftovers to take to Grandpa," she explained. "It's not all for me."

"Right..." Claron squeezed her knee and Rhea jumped at the tickle and swatted him.

"It is. He specifically asked me for some of Conor's pizza."

"Oh Roland," Conor shook his head. "I'll make your pizza a small, Rhea, and deliver him his very own fresh one. Only the best for Roland."

"That's sweet, Conor. Thank you."

"Aye." He held up the note pad. "I'll be getting these worked up for you. Yell if you need me."

"You could join us, Conor," Chloe invited. "If you have some minutes to spare."

Surprised by the invitation, he shifted on his feet under the eyes of everyone else at the table.

"That be right kind of you, Chloe. Best check on the mammy first, but I may swing back by for a round." He hurried off.

"What was that about?" Layla asked.

"What?" Chloe looked confused.

"You. Asking Conor to join us."

"He is a friend, it was only a kind gesture."

"And that it was," Riley agreed.

"Still odd." Layla mumbled.

"You still in a fit, sister?" Claron asked, looking at Layla. "You and Gage on the outs?"

"No. Gage and I are fine." She flicked her hair over her shoulder and straightened in her seat as the door to the restaurant opened and several men walked inside. Chloe and Rhea exchanged a knowing glance that did not go unnoticed by Heidi. "Just curious about Chloe's sudden interest in Conor."

"'Tis not an interest. He be a friend, Layla. Always has been. Hate to see him serving all of us."

"He works here," Layla pointed out.

"Aye, but how many times do you find a sit with friends at the café while you are working? It be the same thing. A small break for him." Chloe turned her focus towards Rhea. "So, where will you be located later this afternoon?"

"What do you mean?"

"Will you be at the B&B? Or at Clary's?"

"B&B, why?"

"I may or may not have a delivery for you."

"Me?" Rhea, hand on her chest, looked to Claron. "I'm getting flowers?" She kissed him sweetly on the lips and he smiled.

"Thanks for that." He winked. "But they are not from me." He looked to his younger sister for answers.

"Seems our Murphy has plans to butter you up," Chloe admitted.

"Murphy?" Rhea, Claron, Riley, and Layla all asked at the same time and had Chloe laughing.

"Aye." She held up her hands. "I do not know his motives. He just wished to send Rhea some flowers."

"Hmm..." Rhea leaned back in her chair against Claron's arm draped behind her. "What could Murphy need or want?"

"Now that is unfair," Riley said. "He could just be wanting to dote upon you, lass."

"His brother's girlfriend?" Thinking it doubtful, Rhea narrowed her gaze at Riley and he shrugged.

"'Tis Murphy," Claron stated. "He's definitely up to something."

"I've sent Rhea flowers before," Riley pointed out. "I had no ulterior motive other than to cheer her up."

"That was after Oliver. Doesn't count." Claron held Rhea's hand. "I bet he's wanting to use me cottage and thinks you can convince me."

Rhea snapped. "That's it. Guarantee it."

"Use your cottage?" Heidi asked.

"To rent it out to tourists," Claron explained. "He and Layla have it in their minds that people would pay to spend time there."

"As they do. 'Tis proven to be a lucrative and good idea," Layla chimed in.

"For you," Claron added.

"And you. We split our profits." Layla's voice rose and everyone at the table tried to quiet her tone. She huffed as her eyes wandered to the table of men across the room. She flashed a dazzling smile.

"Perhaps it's an offer you can't refuse, brother." Riley relaxed in his chair and draped his arm behind Heidi. "Sweet talkin' your lass first..." Riley grinned. "He's smart, our Murphy."

"I'm not complaining." Rhea leaned further into Claron. "I get flowers."

"From a handsome man," Heidi added and had Rhea nodding in agreement.

"Hey, no talk of me brother being handsome," Claron warned her. "Now I must find a way to outdo him. Can't have him wooing my lass."

Rhea rubbed her hands together. "Ooooh... a competition in wooing me. This gets better and better." She nudged Claron and kissed his cheek.

"I could use a good wooing," Chloe admitted and had both brothers groaning. She wriggled her eyebrows. "Come now Riley and Clary, it could be worse." She eyed her sister. "I could be trying to woo your friends."

"Please don't." Riley tugged on one of her curls, his hand finding its place back to behind Heidi. "We already have one sister burning bridges for us."

"Burning bridges. Please." Layla scoffed. "They be the ones not man enough to face me after we end things."

Riley tensed, and Rhea tilted her head and held him with a firm stare. He held up his free hand to show that he was going to remain cool.

Heidi turned towards him with an inquisitive look and he slightly shook his head for her not to ask.

Conor emerged with their orders and began placing them on the table. He leaned forward to slide Rhea her pizza, his elbow knocking over Layla's water. She gasped as the cold liquid landed in her lap and she hopped to her feet. "Conor, you eejit!" She grabbed the first available glass and tossed it all over him.

Dumbfounded, Conor's beard dripped as he stared wide eyed at Layla. "Truly sorry there, Layla. I didn't mean to—"

"Shush!" Layla held her hand in his face and then snatched her purse. "I'm leaving. Find me when you get to the B&B." She cast Conor one last look of disgust as she stormed outside towards her car.

They all watched as she sped away in a whirl of red as her little car zoomed down the street, tires squealing as she went.

Conor held a hand to his chest and looked to the table. "I am very—"

Riley held up his hand. "Do not apologize, Conor. Layla needed to cool off. Come, join us if you can."

"Oh," he reached towards Chloe's hands as she attempted to mop up the spill on the table with napkins. He grabbed the soggy cloths and laid them on his tray. "I got this now, Chloe. So sorry if it spilt on your pretty blouse."

"I'm fine." Chloe continued to help and Heidi handed her more napkins.

Conor's red face slowly faded as he hurried away to toss the ruined napkins and to grab more.

"I think it's more than just a tizzy she's going through." Rhea looked to Riley and Claron. "Layla's been in a terrible mood for over a week."

"She and Gage aren't working out," Chloe stated. "I bumped into him at O'Malley's the other day buying crisps. He mentioned his plans of moving on. I believe it may have happened, though Layla's too prideful to admit it. I think she really cared for him."

"That explains a lot." Rhea took a sip of her drink. "Hate that for her."

"I don't." Riley accepted the slap to his thigh from Heidi.

"That's not very nice," she chided.

"There's more to this story than you know, lass. I'm glad Gage grew wise. Let us hope we still have a friend, brother." He motioned towards Claron as he took a sip of his drink.

"He spoke to me freely, so I do not see why he wouldn't remain friends with you two," Chloe pointed out.

"True. There is hope. Guess we will see at the pub tonight."

"You're going to the pub tonight?" Heidi asked, turning to face Riley.

He tucked a bit of her hair behind her ear and leaned forward. "Care to join me?"

Rhea bit back a smile as she saw Heidi swallow at Riley's nearness.

"Um, sure. That is, if Rhea doesn't already have plans for us."

"The pub it is." Rhea toasted towards them.

"Brilliant." Riley brushed his knuckle over Heidi's cheek. "I demand a spin or two on the dance floor, Heidi love. Don't let Conor bewitch you all night."

Everyone chuckled at that thought.

Heidi met him stare for stare. "You can have me for however many dances you want, Riley O'Rifcan." And she felt pure satisfaction at the slight glint in his eyes that accepted her challenge.

«CHAPTER SIX»

Riley pulled into the drive of the B&B after pit stopping at O'Malley's Market for his mam. Due to Tom's gossiping, he was an hour behind on his mental schedule of visiting with his parents and then heading to the pub. As he entered, Roland and his parents sat in the sitting room.

"Hello to the house," he called in greeting.

"Ah, Riley, boyo," his father beamed at him. "Haven't seen yer face in these parts for several days. How be Galway?"

"Busy, frustrating, and absolutely horrid." Riley forced a smile as he reached over Roland's shoulder and shook his hand. "Roland, good to see you."

"And you." Rhea's grandpa nudged his glasses up his nose as he set his crossword puzzle down in his lap.

"And what you be up to, love?" Mrs. O'Rifcan asked. "Thought you'd be heading to the local for a pint or two."

"That's me plan. Got a wee bit sidetracked by Tom O'Malley."

"Ah," Roland chuckled. "He's in a chatty mood the last few days. Prepping for the flower festival has him all worked up now that he's on the committee."

"So it would seem," Riley agreed. He looked to Roland. "Rhea about?"

"No." Roland sighed happily. "She is at Clary's cottage. Though they plan to be at Murphy's this evening."

"And what of Heidi?" Riley asked.

Sidna's brow rose and she cast a pointed gaze at her husband. He shook his head and bit back a smile at his wife's pleasure of her son seeking out the new woman in town.

"She left not a half hour ago. Set out on her own, she did. Determined to shop the stores before heading to the pub."

"By herself?" Riley asked. "Chloe and Layla not tag along?"

"Chloe be helping the McCarthy's at the restaurant. Conor needed to run a few deliveries and his mam was short-handed. Layla be dolling up for the pub."

"Of course she is." Riley's grim expression had Sidna pointing to the sofa so he could tell them what was on his mind. "Did anyone tell you how she treated Conor today?"

"Rhea did. I'm ashamed for it. Layla should not react the way she did, especially to sweet Conor, bless him." Sidna shifted her yarn and began to knit a new row. Pearl stitch. Knit stitch. Pearl stitch. Knit stitch. Riley watched her movements; the brisk and efficient pace had her completing two new rows before he responded.

"Aye. She has a nasty cloud above her head at the moment. She despises Heidi. Hasn't even tried to welcome her."

"It's another pretty lass drawing attention away from the lads." Sidna shrugged.

"She did not act this way when Rhea came to town." Riley pointed out.

"That be because Rhea had a glad eye for Clary from the start." Mrs. O'Rifcan's face split into a joyous smile. "She was not competition."

"True enough. But Heidi just be after making friends. I hate to see my own sister so hateful towards her."

"Layla will come around," Mr. O'Rifcan, Claron Senior, said. "She's always in a mood after one of her relationships fails."

"Aye." Riley ran a hand through his hair. "Well, I guess since everyone has already run off, I best amble along to the pub. Murphy will have some cheer to share, I'm sure."

"Indeed he will." Sidna smiled tenderly at him. "Be sure to show Heidi a good time, love. She seemed tired today... or bored. Not sure which."

"I intend to, Mam. She be ready for some fun. Let us hope between the lot of us we can make it so."

"I believe you can. Now go. Off with you. Be young and dance the night away."

He rose, walked to his mother and kissed her cheek. "Night to you all."

"Have a care, love," his mother called after him as he set out the door and up the footpath towards Murphy's.

He'd left his truck at the B&B and enjoyed walking the few blocks in the open air. He needed the slow pace of Castlebrook after a busy week. He'd drafted three different sets of plans for his client in Galway, and it looked as if the final sketch would be the winner. He took into consideration some of Heidi's feedback and felt he'd settled upon a crisp and clean design mixed with local flair. The new hurdle would be finding a contractor willing to take on such a complex project. He'd do it, though. It was his job, and he loved it. And, thank heavens, he was good at it. He'd just have to buckle down, no distractions, and reach out to some of his best connections.

He narrowed his eyes as he spotted Heidi opening the door to Murphy's Pub a block up. She was easy to spot, all leg and elegant strut. She'd have every man eating out of the palm of her hand tonight, he was sure of it. That is, if his sister did not make Heidi's night a living nightmare. Perplexed over Layla's sour mood the last several days, he focused on seeing Heidi. His sister needed to come to terms with the fact she was not the only female in the world. Tough pill to swallow for Layla, he knew, but to treat Heidi the way she had was ridiculous.

He stopped in front of the door and quickly assessed his appearance in the glass. Combing a hand through his hair and adjusting his shoulders, he reached for the door handle.

"Hold the door there, Riley." Conor walked up, his restaurant attire changed to a pressed shirt of pale green that made his red hair flair like a siren as he rushed forward, adjusting the waist band on his pants to accommodate his burly middle.

"You clean up nicely, Conor." Riley leaned towards him and sniffed. "Bit of perfume, have we?"

Conor laughed. "Aye." He rubbed his hands together as he stepped through the open door. "The lasses enjoy a nice smelling lad."

"Do they now?" Riley quirked an eyebrow as he lifted his shirt front to smell. "I'm afraid I did not apply me own. Perhaps it is your night tonight, my friend."

Conor shook his head. "The day I best Riley O'Rifcan at attracting bonny lasses will be the day I find me grave."

Riley offered a firm and friendly pat on Conor's back as they walked up to the bar.

Conor slammed his hand down to draw Murphy's attention their way. "A pint, Murphy," he called. "I've got a throat on me."

Murphy waved in acknowledgment as he topped off two orders on the other end of the bar.

"Aye, I need a whiskey." Riley slid under the bar's counter-hinged door. No stranger to helping his brother out behind the bar, he quickly grabbed a glass and began filling it with Guinness for Conor, followed by a whiskey for himself. Before he could even think of looking for Heidi, he found himself filling several more drinks for other customers and soon found himself stuck behind the bar for what looked to be a long night.

∞

"Don't look now, love, but I believe me brother has finally arrived." Murphy slid a martini to Heidi and she leaned to the left just enough to see past Murphy's shoulder and find Riley serving the other end of the bar.

"See, he doesn't even come down here to say hello." She shrugged.

Murphy swiped his towel over the counter top. Having listened to Heidi's complaints about Riley for the last ten minutes, he found himself amused that his brother was running scared.

"He's avoiding me because I asked him out."

Murphy's eyes widened at that announcement. "You asked him for a night out? And he said no?"

She nodded. "Sort of. I basically told him I planned for him to take me out. That I wanted him to."

"And?"

"Nothing. He's been slightly avoiding me. Well, we sat by one another at lunch today, but it wasn't the same."

"Forgive him, Heidi, for he is a complete eejit. Lost his mind, he has. I never thought I'd see the day Riley O'Rifcan ran scared from a woman."

Her lips tilted into a small smile before she covered it by taking a sip of her drink.

"Why if you walked into me pub and said, "Murphy, I have a glad eye for ye. What say you about that?" I'd say alright, my love. Yes, my goddess of the Amazons, my heart is yours.""

Heidi burst into laughter and Murphy wriggled his eyebrows at her.

"Amazon goddess? Am I that vicious?"

"Oh no. Not vicious. Beautiful. A warrior goddess, you are, dear Heidi. Strong. And by the end of the night you'll be completely in love with me." He winked as he dried a glass and stacked it under the counter.

"You think so?"

"Aye. Though there be plenty of lads upset that I be taking you off the market, I must do my duty."

"And what duty is that?" she asked, amused.

"To serve the goddess, of course."

She shook her head and chuckled. "You flatter me too much, Murphy. I'm just a simple girl from Texas."

"Ah, a rustler from Texas. Heidi Rustler, the long-legged bewitching goddess that sets men's hearts to racing. I like it." He affirmed his description with a concise nod.

"One day, Murphy O'Rifcan, a woman is going to waltz in here and completely shake up your world if you keep spouting sonnets like that."

Grinning, Murphy slid away down the bar to hear a customer's order. She watched as he laughed and made a joking comment back to the patron before greeting another woman with a kiss to the hand. *He's a dangerous one*, she thought. Much like Riley. All the O'Rifcan men really. Charming. Handsome. She saw Jace standing amongst some friends across the bar. His hair, dark like Riley's, was cut short and trim compared to the unruly mass that helped behind the bar. He offered a friendly wave. She smiled in greeting as her eyes continued to circle around the room. She spotted Claron and Rhea walking into the pub and found herself sighing to herself at the sweetness of the two. Claron was smitten with her friend, completely lost in Rhea. And that was how it should be, she reminded herself. Love was to shake you up, knock you off your feet, and then leave you breathless. It was meant to completely transform you. Wasn't it?

She spun back towards the bar top when she heard someone tapping her glass. When she faced forward, Riley stood before her. "Getting a bit empty there, lass. Need a refill?"

He patiently waited for her to answer, a hand towel tossed over his shoulder and a disarming grin on his face.

"Sure." She slid her glass to him. He disposed of it and quickly placed a fresh one on top of the counter and hastily whipped up another martini.

She took a slow sip. "Don't tell Murphy, but I think yours is better."

"It's all the practice I get, sipping fancy drinks in Galway all week. Murphy, bless him, isn't as well traveled." He smirked as she raised a brow over the top of her glass.

"I'm surprised you're speaking to me."

"And why is that?" Confused, his brow furrowed as he crossed his arms and stared at her.

"You've been avoiding me, Riley, admit it."

"I sat with you just today, lass."

"Sat with, yes. Spoke to..." She shrugged. "Not really."

"I promise I meant no offense, love."

She set her glass down on the bar. "It's funny, I don't really believe you."

Baffled that he'd made her feel so low, Riley tossed his towel onto the bar top and ducked under the counter door. He popped up next to Heidi and held out his hand. "'Twas not my intention to make you feel this way, Heidi. Come, let me give you a spin or two."

She took one last sip of her drink and then slid her hand in his.

She liked the feel of his hand. The warmth, the wide palm, the long fingers wrapped around hers. She also liked the way he swung her out at arm's length before pulling her into a spin and back into his manly frame. He tugged her close, as the dance floor was crowded, but she hoped it was because he wished to as well. He smelled fresh and clean, as if he'd just showered and walked through a warm breeze to reach the pub. She indulged by lightly resting her head against his shoulder and enjoying the closeness. The tempo slowed, and instead of breaking away, he adjusted their speed and held her close.

"You have a grand day in Castlebrook?" His chest rumbled against her ear as he spoke and she briefly looked up to find him staring down at her. When their eyes met, she paused a moment in her steps. *So blue*, she thought. Depthless and piercing, yet kind beneath the surface. "Heidi?" He shifted uncomfortably and she blinked.

"Oh, yes. Yes, I did. I saw Angel's Gap again. Rhea carried on about fairies for over half an hour. She really needs to stop reading those books. I saw Clary's fields. Seems they are on their way to a good harvest. His words, not mine." She reached up to brush a stray hair from her face and then rested her hand on his shoulder once more. "And your mother filled my stomach to the brim with delicious food and drink. So yeah, it hasn't been half bad."

"I'm glad."

"And your day?" she asked. "Was it good?"

"It had its moments." He lightly spun her away from him and brought her back into his arms. The hand at the small of her back lifted and he lightly played with the tips of her long hair. "You look magnificent tonight, has anyone told you?"

"Only Murphy."

"Ah, he'd be one to notice as well. A keen eye, our Murphy."

"You look rather dashing yourself."

"Why thank you. I had a pretty lass to impress." He winked at her.

"I see." She spun outward again and bumped into Gage. He offered a quick smile in welcome at the two of them.

The song ended and as Riley began to speak, Gage tapped on Heidi's shoulder. "Do me the honor, Heidi?" he asked.

Heidi looked at Riley and waited for a reaction. Resigned that he did not seem to care, she forced a polite smile. "Sure. Thank you for the dance, Riley." She squeezed his hand, but he did not release it. "Riley?"

He lightly tugged her back towards him, his eyes never leaving Gage. "How about we walk a bit?"

Heidi looked between the two men, trying to read their emotions. Gage seemed unoffended, but Riley radiated restrained anger. "My sister will be arriving soon," Riley told him.

Gage's brow rose. "Layla? Tonight?"

"Aye."

"I doubt she'd want to see me." Gage held up a hand to hold off Riley's wrath. "Don't blame me for her doing."

"What?" Riley stiffened. "You're the one who's ended things."

"That be a lie, I'm afraid. Layla ended things with me a couple days ago. Something about wanting to experience other possibilities."

Riley's shoulders relaxed, and he shook Gage's hand. "Sorry, lad. She's been playing the victim. I just assumed."

"Yes, well... it would never have worked out any way. Odd, dating my mate's sister. It didn't sit well."

Riley laughed. "Glad to hear that. You'd be the first to say it."

Heidi slid her arm around Riley's waist as she waited patiently for the two friends to finish.

"Now are you going to share the pretty lass or not, Riley?" Gage asked, nodding towards Heidi.

"That would be a no." Riley patted Gage on the shoulder as he began leading Heidi off the dance floor.

"You aren't going to let me dance with him?"

Riley looked down at her. "No."

"And why not?" She slid to a stop and he acted annoyed as he lightly tucked her hair behind her ear.

"Because tonight, dear Heidi, you are mine."

"Not if I have anything to say about it." Conor walked up, an overly vigorous pat to Riley's back that had him flinching. Heidi bit back a smile as Conor draped his arm over her shoulders. "I steal her for one dance, Riley. Just one. Then you can have her, hmm? After all, you said it earlier, tonight's me night." He toasted his pint towards Riley.

Heidi slipped from Riley's grasp as Conor's massive hand clamped down over hers. "Come, Heidi, let me give you a twirl."

She had absolutely no say, but she found Conor's excitement rubbing off on her. She cast a glance over her shoulder at Riley and he shrugged with a regretful smile before chuckling. She watched as he made his way back to the bar, his eyes ever watchful as she began dodging Conor's missteps.

∞

His intention for slipping behind the bar was to retrieve his own drink, not to be trapped and filling orders for the entire pub. It's what he deserved for not being patient. The pub was always crowded when a live band played, and Murphy was much like Clary in that he never had enough hands on deck to help with the work. So, he filled another pint, slid it to an awaiting hand, and immediately worked on another while keeping a knowing eye on Heidi's whereabouts.

Currently, she sat with Rhea, Clary, Conor, and Chloe, and a grumpy Layla who toyed with the straw in her drink. She laughed as Conor threw his arm around Chloe's shoulders and sloppily kissed his sister's temple. Chloe playfully rolled her eyes and nudged her elbow in Conor's side, their good friend easing back to his normal relaxed posture. Conor was a great friend, to all of them, and his joy for life and friends made everyone around him comfortable and happy. Heidi appeared relaxed and for the first time since her arrival, content. And he believed he owed much of that to Conor's easygoing presence.

Heidi glanced up and caught Riley staring at her. She flashed a quick smile and winked at him as she stood with the others. They were leaving. Disappointment raged within him as he debated abandoning Murphy. But loyalty won out and he knew he could not leave his brother to fend off all the greedy hands himself.

Clary walked over and reached a hand across the bar. Riley grabbed it in a tight hand shake. "See the women home for me, brother?"

"Of course." Claron grinned. "I could think of no better pleasure."

"And I will be assisting." Conor set his empty glass on the bar top, Riley swooping it away and then shaking his friend's hand.

"Always the helpful one when a pretty lass is involved, is our Conor." Clary patted Conor on the back as they turned to head towards the door. Riley waved to the group and turned to start filling glasses on the tap.

Heidi slipped away from the group and ducked under the bar counter and popped up beside him. He jumped as she appeared beside him, taking him off guard. She smiled as he slipped the drinks across the counter and wiped up any spills in their wake. He flung the towel over his shoulder, and Murphy slipped behind them, offering Heidi a quick kiss on the cheek in passing as he high fived a friend at the bar before taking another drink order.

"That brother of mine." Riley just shook his head.

"He's charming." Heidi reached up and straightened his collar. "Goodnight, handsome." She rose on her tip toes and kissed his cheek, making sure she held his gaze a moment afterward. "Should you be in Castlebrook tomorrow, I'll be at the B&B."

Riley ignored the shouts and hand pounds on the bar as he focused only upon Heidi. She devastated him, in the most incredible way, and that had his nerves jumping. He cleared his throat. "I'm sorry I've been occupied tonight." She held a finger to his lips, that move alone causing his heart to squeeze a smidgen more.

"No need to apologize. You've been a help for Murphy. The fact you sacrificed your night of fun to help your brother just makes me like you more." She winked at him.

He shifted on his feet and she chuckled. "Gotta get used to me saying it, Riley." She kissed his cheek again. "I'm an honest woman."

"Of that, I have no doubt." He tapped her nose. "Have a care, lass. I'll be seeing you."

"You bet you will." She tossed a wave at Murphy and ducked back under the bar and scurried over to an awaiting Rhea. He caught the curious glance of Rhea and shrugged. She draped her arm over Heidi's shoulders as they turned towards an awaiting Claron holding the door open. As he watched them leave, his distraction cost him a towel pop to the arm as Murphy attempted to break his frozen reverie.

«CHAPTER SEVEN»

"It's all about the release," Rhea explained and then demonstrated. She lightly whisked the fly into the air, back over her shoulder until her line was nearly straight, then swished her arm forward. The line graced the top of the water and within moments Rhea snagged a fish.

Heidi glanced at the fly fishing rod in her hands. "This is ridiculous." She set it aside and reached for what she deemed a "regular" rod and reel.

"Don't give up yet," Rhea chuckled as she tied the fish onto a separate line and plunged the day's catches back into the cool water for safe keeping.

"Not all of us can perform with such grace," Layla called from across the bank.

Rhea laughed and watched as Chloe cast her line into the water and sat on the green grass and waited patiently for a bite.

"She always was a show off," Heidi mocked, accepting the sassy head tilt from Rhea with a smile. "I wonder if I could catch them with my hands."

"I would love to see that," Rhea baited. "Trout are fickle creatures, Heidi. You don't want to scare them off."

"I'm sure I can manage." She slipped her shoes and socks off and began hopping from stone to stone across the river, the water playfully lapping against her calves. She rolled the hem of her shirt up and tied it in a knot at the center of her back and pulled her hair into a quick bun on top of her head.

"'Tis getting serious now," Layla teased. "Hair is up."

All the women smiled as they watched Heidi begin to stalk through the shallow water to find her prey.

"So Layla, are you ever going to tell us what happened with Gage?" Rhea asked, gracefully casting her line again.

"What is there to tell? It did not work out."

"You seemed pretty crazy about him."

"He was looking for something serious," Layla explained.

"And you aren't?" Heidi asked curiously.

Layla eyed the new American and her eyes lost their usual sting. "Not really," she answered honestly. "Is it wrong for me to just want a lad to treat me to a meal every now and then? To snog me in the moonlight and say sweet things? I'm not after a marriage. I'm not after a long-term relationship. I just want a bit of fun. Gage is not built for flirtations. He's built for commitment."

"Not the usual reputation a man gets." Heidi was impressed.

"Aye, 'tis an honorable trait to be sure, but not one I'm after at the moment."

"Too bad you're kin to all the other good looking men in this town." Pity laced Heidi's voice as Chloe burst into laughter behind her.

"Is that not the truth?" Chloe asked. "Seems the pickings are slim here in Castlebrook. Heaven knows how I will ever settle down one day. I never leave."

"You will find a wonderful man one day, Chloe." Rhea looked at the youngest O'Rifcan sister with a warm smile.

"Oh I don't doubt it, just might take a while."

"Perhaps I should enlist your Aunt Grace to help me, Rhea," Layla smirked. "She seems to pick them just fine. Trips to Fiji and the like."

"Still... I think your mother is the best matchmaker I know," Rhea added. "She's relentless. Like a bull."

Guffawing with laughter, all the woman startled when a deep voice rang out behind them.

"All these beautiful women wading in the water... pure sirens." Murphy grinned as he walked up and set his tackle box on the soft grass next to Rhea. "Can a lonely man join such beauty for a bit of fishing?"

"Blast, Murphy!" An angrier voice carried their way as Jaron, the brother whose coloring most favored Claron, stormed up with several rods in his grip. "You stole me rod, brother. I'm not using your sorry excuses here. Trade now." He held the rods out and Murphy shrugged, completely fine with using whatever rod was given to him. Jaron then nodded a welcome to the women. "Nice to see you all. 'Tis a pretty day. Seems we all had the same idea."

"You're welcome to join me in the water," Heidi called. "I don't know you yet."

Jaron and Murphy exchanged a quick glance. "A beautiful woman in the water, how could I resist that invitation?" Jaron chuckled as he rolled up his pant legs and set his bare feet on the rocks and walked out towards Heidi.

"Careful lad, could be a trap," Murphy called to his brother.

"Then I'd consider myself lucky to be ensnared by such a beauty."

Chloe and Layla both rolled their eyes as Rhea giggled and shook her head in mock dismay. "You O'Rifcans and your charm. Seriously... kills me."

"It's a gift." Riley ducked under the tree line and rested a hand on Rhea's shoulder so as not to scare her with his approach. "Look at you lass, such finesse."

"Makes us all look bad." Layla held up her rod and reel. "Clearly, Roland and Rhea only fly fish to make us all feel inadequate."

Rhea threw back her head and laughed.

"Seems our Heidi is teaching Jaron the Texas way." Riley watched as his brother and Heidi plunged their hands into the water and scrambled.

"She's not patient enough for fishing," Rhea commented. "And Jaron is just humoring her. He's a good sport. What brings you here?"

He pointed at his rod.

"I meant that I thought you would be at your place or in Galway."

"'Tis the weekend. I wanted to see me family."

"I see."

"And I helped Clary with his fields today. He's wrapping it up now. I was only getting in the way. Particular about his machines, he is."

"You're particular about your tools as well. I've seen your desk. All your pencils are sharpened to the exact same length." She motioned a hand in front of her in a straight line.

Riley laughed. "You noticed that?"

"Kind of hard not to," she snickered as he knuckled her shoulder. "But I'm sure he appreciates your help."

"Aye. He needs another hand, but he's too stubborn to admit he needs one."

"He knows he does. More like he's too frugal to invest in one."

Riley pointed at her. "Perhaps one day, when a certain lass has a say over some of those finances, maybe she can convince him of that investment."

"Perhaps one day, when a certain lass is waiting for him at home, he will find need of that investment all on his own so as to spend more time with her," Rhea replied.

"Bang on!" Riley laughed. "That most certainly is sly and smart, Rhea love. Clary doesn't stand a chance."

Heidi's head popped up at the sound of Riley's laugh and she waved in greeting.

"Looking good, lass! Teach Jaron your ways. He needs all the help he can get."

Jaron patted Heidi on the back as he waded back towards the bank. "You hop in brother, Heidi be a good teacher. Real good with her hands." Jaron winked and spoke conspiratorially as if Rhea weren't there. Rhea kicked her foot out and splashed him. "Only kidding." He sat on the bank and watched as Heidi continued her quest to catch fish with her bare hands.

"Go," Rhea whispered, urging him to venture into the water.

Riley's face grew serious.

"I can tell you want to," Rhea continued.

"Right now, I'm just enjoying the view."

She shoved his shoulder and he cackled. "Fine, I'm going. Don't have to twist me arm, lass." He playfully kissed Rhea's cheek as he rolled up his pant legs and set out towards Heidi.

"You're quite a sight out here in the water." Riley accepted the friendly hug she gave him, her wet hand patting him on the back.

"It feels incredible. Kind of cold when you first step in, but it's nice."

"And have you caught any fish yet?"

"No. Jaron and I were close, but no cigar."

Riley laughed jovially. "Perhaps you just need a different O'Rifcan brother to help you."

"Well, line'em up," Heidi teased. She placed a hand on her heart. "Oh, were you talking about you?" She batted her lashes in jest. "My mistake."

He pushed her shoulder and she teetered on the rock she stood upon. "Easy there, you're currently my favorite. I'd hate for you to ruin that."

"I'm everyone's favorite." He struggled to keep his own balance as she shoved him in return.

"Wait," she held up her hand for him to pause in their shoving match and pointed into the water. "There's a trout."

She bent her knees and slowly made her way through the water, Riley tight on her heels. It was hard to concentrate with him so close, his hands inches from hers as they both plunged into the water at the same time. She felt the sleek and slimy feel of a squirmy fish as she raised her hands. Riley held one side of it as well. Cheering, they raised it above their heads and everyone along the bank hooted in celebration. Heidi beamed up at Riley. She gasped as her foot slipped and she stumbled forward. Riley released his grip on the fish and grabbed for Heidi's waist as she started to fall. Their feet tangled amongst each other while slipping on the rocky river bottom and sent them both heading straight for the water. Riley pulled and twisted at the last second, Heidi squealing as they landed with a splash.

Laughter rang along the bank as she came up for air, her head resting on top of Riley's chest. He raised his head, his hair sleeked back and groaned having taken the brunt of the fall against the rocks. "You okay?" She swiped her hair from her eyes as it clung to her cheeks. A deep rumble released from his lips as he burst into laughter and pointed to her hands between them. She looked down and squealed again as spotted glassy eyes peered at her in utter desperation. "Bleh!" She tossed the fish aside and rinsed her hands in the water as she slowly pushed off of Riley and stood. She offered him a hand.

"A couple of wet rats." Murphy lowered his head as he laughed.

"That's what you get for horsin' around," Rhea called, her wide smile flashing in the sun.

Heidi tugged on her wet shirt, suddenly feeling a bit self-conscious. Riley tugged her hand. "Come lass, Mam will see to us." He pulled her to the opposite bank closest to the back door of the B&B.

∞

"Mam!" Riley called, as he entered the B&B. They stepped into the kitchen and his mother sat at the small dinette table with a friend sipping tea. She turned at their entry and spit her sip back into her cup, her eyes wide. "Riley O'Rifcan!" she scolded. "You come to spend the day with our sweet Heidi and you drag her through the river? A son should know better." She clicked her tongue as she stood to her feet and began nudging Heidi to a seat of her own. "Heidi, this is the Mrs. O'Malley from the market."

Heidi nodded in greeting as she started to stand again, but Sidna placed a forceful hand on her shoulder to remain seated. "Let me have a look at ye." She eyed them both and her gaze narrowed on Riley before she popped him upside the head.

"Ouch. And what was that for?" he asked.

"For bein' a fool, Riley O'Rifcan. Treatin' our Heidi in such a way. Why, I thought you had more sense when it came to treating a woman respectably."

Riley opened his mouth to respond and she shushed him. "Heidi dear, I'll make you a nice hot cup of tea. Actually, no. Riley will make you a hot cup of tea while I fetch you a towel." She eyed her son sternly and he walked to the cupboards to retrieve two cups and to obey his mother. She bustled off, Mrs. O'Malley biting back a grin as she eyed Riley making his way around the kitchen.

"And how be Tom, Mrs. O'Malley? Plannin' for the flower festival?" Riley asked, as he poured boiling water over tea bags and walked towards the table. He slid a cup to Heidi.

"Oh, he's in a tizzy about it, he is. Enjoys working with Chloe, though. Splendid gem, she is. Patient as the day is long."

"I'm sure between the two of them Castlebrook will have a grand time."

123

"Aye, I believe so too. Though I won't be sad when it is over." She sipped her tea as Sidna walked back in and tossed a towel at Riley. She then opened Heidi's towel and gently draped it over her shoulders.

Heidi grinned as Riley began toweling off his hair. "Just so you know, Mam, it was not my fault, falling in the river. Heidi pushed me."

Heidi's eyes widened. "That is a blatant lie," she challenged. "My foot slipped. You're the one who grabbed me and made me lose my complete balance."

"I was trying to save you from such a fate as this." He waved his hand over his wet shirt. "And what thanks do I get but the same fate and a scolding from the mammy. I was a perfect gentleman, I was, Mam. You have me word. Heidi here—" he tisked his tongue as she reached over and slapped his arm with a loud pop, her flushed cheeks telling him she was embarrassed.

Sidna hooted with laughter as she settled in her seat again.

"'Tis a fine man who's willing to sacrifice himself to catch a beautiful woman."

"Aye. You'd think she'd be more grateful," Riley teased.

"I am grateful. Though you made me lose my fish."

"That fish is grateful," he amended and they both grinned at one another thinking of the poor creature smushed between them.

"Speaking of fish, you both smell like one. Perhaps you can wash up so as not to bathe the whole house in the stench." Sidna waved them on.

Riley stood and turned. Heidi froze. "Riley!" She hurried towards him and her hands tenderly touched his back.

"What?" he asked, turning, concern in his face as he lifted Heidi's chin. "What be the matter, love? You alright?" He turned her chin in his hands to inspect her for injury and she just shook her head. "Your back. It's bleeding."

He straightened, and his mother walked over and lifted his shirt. "Aye, boyo, nasty cuts here and there. Goodness me." She lowered his shirt and pointed to the sitting room. "I'll get my kit. Splay yourself on the couch love, I'll see to you."

"I'm fine." Riley waved away their concern. "The rocks gave me a wee snag. Nothing a hot shower can't fix. I'll steal the suite that Clary uses from time to time. I have me a duffle in the truck with some extra clothes." He noted both women's concern and smiled tenderly, bringing them both in for a group hug. "'Tis nice to have such fine women worry over me."

"Go." Sidna planted a loud kiss on his cheek before pulling away. "The two of you. Shower and clean up. I'll bring your bag up and leave it on the bed. If your back be bothering you after, I'll tend to it."

"Thanks, Mam." He kissed her in return, and with his arm still draped over Heidi's shoulders, led her up the back stairwell.

«CHAPTER EIGHT»

She sighed as she reached the top of the landing and stood before her door. "I'm sorry about your back."

Riley shrugged. "'Twas a necessary battle wound. I did not want you to suffer the likes of this."

Heidi stepped towards him and his smile slowly faded, his eyes grew serious. She gently brushed her fingertips over the light stubble that graced his cheek. "It was kind, Riley, and a sweet gesture. Chivalrous, if I need to keep going."

He diverted his gaze and she nudged his face so he looked at her once more. "You're a good man, Riley O'Rifcan."

She leaned up and lightly brushed her lips over his cheek. "Thank you." She slipped away and turned the knob to her room.

"I'll be waiting for you in the kitchen, lass," Riley stated, standing at his own door.

Heidi turned and a slow smile tugged at her lips. "Have you not had enough of me for one day?"

"Though it worries me, no. Not near enough."

His honesty had them both standing in contemplation and staring at one another.

"Something to think on then." Heidi turned and walked into her room and shut the door.

She released the pent-up breath from her lungs as she leaned against the door. The man was a conundrum. One minute he ignored her, or at the least, wanted to ignore her. And the next, he's batting those pretty blue eyes at her. Okay, maybe he wasn't batting. Smoldering. Yes, definitely smoldering at her. So what was she to make of him? Rhea had bragged on Riley so much so that Heidi had built up a rather impressive image of him. He delivered. And as her time ticked by in Ireland, she could only think of one thing that she wished to experience. It wasn't castles or the Cliffs of Mohr. It was Riley. To know him. Baffled that she was even thinking of spending what little time in beautiful Ireland that she had pursuing a man, her thoughts had her trudging to the shower to wash away the smell of fish and shaking her head in dismay.

A hot shower did wonders for her mood. It also helped that Layla had left her some invigorating bath scrubs that the sister had created herself. Layla was gifted, that was for sure, as she ran the loofa over her shoulders. The smell of jasmine and gardenia scented the steamy air as she rinsed off and stepped out to dry off. She stifled a scream as Rhea sat on the toilet, legs crossed, flipping through a magazine.

Heidi tucked the towel around her. "It's a good thing I wasn't naked."

Rhea waved her hand as if she didn't care.

"What are you doing up here?"

"Waiting for you." She looked up then and turned the magazine towards Heidi. "Did you see this dress? Super cute." She dogeared the page and flipped onward.

"Rhea..." Heidi prodded. "What are you really doing up here? Because I know it's not to read my magazine."

"Just wanted to check on you. Riley's in the kitchen. Said he was waiting on you."

"He did plan to, yes."

"What do you two have planned?"

"You would have to ask him."

Rhea tilted her head and studied Heidi as she towel-dried her hair. She closed the magazine and tossed it onto the vanity. "I proposed the idea you two come to the cottage for supper, but he shot that idea down, said he planned to take you to Galway this evening."

"Galway?" Heidi's brows rose. "That sounds like fun."

"It's a bit of a drive."

"I'm sure he'll have me home before midnight, momma." Heidi winked at her as she lathered herself in one of the lotions Layla had left her as well. "Layla should really sell this stuff. It's fantastic."

"Don't change the subject." Rhea clasped her hands in her lap.

"Are you worried about me? Or upset with me? I can't really tell." Heidi stopped in mid-stroke as she set her brush on the vanity and turned to face her friend. "I won't go if you aren't comfortable with the idea."

"It's not that." Rhea sighed. "I just... I love you both, and I've never seen you act like this over a man, and I have certainly never seen Riley so serious.

He's barely cracked a joke down there, or flirted for that matter. It's not like him."

"Maybe he's just trying to figure me out."

"Maybe." Rhea leaned her chin in her hands. "Both of you deserve the absolute best. I'm just a bit surprised with the two of you, both acting so different than you normally do. It's made me nervous for you both."

"Rhea," Heidi reached over and grabbed her friend's hand. "You came to Ireland to escape Oliver and the horrible situation that transpired between the two of you. Were you expecting to meet a man like Claron? Were you expecting your entire life to change from the moment you stepped foot here?"

"No, but—"

"But you did, and it did. Sometimes we can't control the hand fate deals us."

"What are you saying?"

"I'm saying that Riley O'Rifcan, whether for good or bad, has shaken up my life. Only time— time with him, time here in Ireland, time in Texas— can show me which way it will go. I'm going to Galway. I want to. I want to spend time with him. Not because he's more important than you, because he's not. I just want to get to know more about him to see if these feelings I have are foolish or substantial."

"I understand. And I understand the confusion in the heart and mind as well. I felt it with Claron the moment I saw him. It's odd. It's like a knowing. Deep down. A knowing in the heart that that man could change it all for you. So I will be praying that Galway goes well, because I can't have two of my favorite people hating one another." Rhea squeezed Heidi's hand. "Now, if I were you, I would be sure to wear a slinky little number, a dress that will knock his socks off. Because if I know anything, it's that Riley O'Rifcan will treat you to a nice night out."

"Woo hoo!" Heidi slapped Rhea's thigh and laughed with her as she hopped to her feet. "Then I guess I better start primping."

Rhea walked to the door and paused, her hand on the knob. "I'm glad you're here, Heidi."

Heidi looked up from her makeup bag and smiled. "Me too, Rhea."

"See you downstairs." Rhea slipped out, the door shutting quietly behind her.

∞

"If it be privacy you're after, boyo, I could shoo the rest of the family to the dining hall and have a nice set up here in the kitchen, candles and all." Mrs. O'Rifcan walked over to a cupboard and pulled out a lace table cloth. "Your nanny's fine cloths." She showed it to Riley and he slid his arm around his mother's shoulders and kissed the top of her head.

"'Tis a sweet offer, Mam. But my plan is Galway. I'll be bringing her back here tonight and you can spoil her with a splendid breakfast. How's that?"

"I just don't like the idea of you travelin' so far for a simple meal, when I could whip together somethin' spectacular right here."

"Don't I know it," Riley agreed. "But—"

"But you wish to spoil the lass and make glad eyes at her without your mammy interfering."

"More like without my brothers interfering. But yes, you too." He flinched as she squeezed his side.

"Alright then, me feelings are only hurt a smidgen, but I will let you escape this once."

"Thank you for understanding." He grinned as Claron walked in from the back door. "And here I thought everyone would still be fishing. Not a soul out on the banks." He set his rod to the side of the door.

"You're late to the party, brother," Jaron called while taking a bite out of an apple behind the counter. "Your lass was the main bread winner today. Rhea put us all to shame. Riley and Heidi took a tumble in the water, and Chloe insisted upon the cleaning, though she sweet talked a passing Murphy and Tommy to help her."

"And where be my lass now?" Claron asked.

Jaron shrugged. "That I do not know."

"H,m, and it seemed for a moment that you knew everything."

Jaron grinned. "And don't you forget it, brother." He saluted with his apple as he made his way towards the sitting room, stopping briefly to pat Riley on the shoulder. "Careful, brother. The waters you be treading now be dangerous underfoot." He winked and cringed as his mother popped him upside the head.

"Perhaps you should take lessons from your younger brothers, since they be the ones with pretty lasses."

Jaron slipped out the kitchen door, a bit too eager to escape his mother's lecture on relationships. "Now, Clary," Sidna turned to him. "Rhea is up the stairs with Heidi. I imagine having some womanly chats. You can settle here on the stool and tell me how the farm is faring."

Claron slid into a seat as Riley slipped into the one beside him. "Crops are coming along. Cows are healthy. Can't complain."

"Rhea help you today?" Riley asked. Sorry I did not stick around after afternoon milking."

"She helped for the morning milking, but then she opted for fishing this afternoon. Good thing, it sounds like, otherwise none of us would feast tonight."

"You can have my share. I'll be taking Heidi to Galway."

"That so? That be the cause of Jaron's teasing then."

"Aye." Riley shifted uncomfortably. "Though I must admit, I'm starting to waver a bit."

"You will not go back on your word, lad, or I'll—"

Riley held up his hand towards his mother. "No worries, Mam. I plan to treat Heidi to a splendid evening, just a bit uneasy about it all."

"Then why do it?" Claron asked, taking a sip of water that his mother placed in front of him.

"Good question. And I don't have an answer for ye, brother. Just feels like I should."

"She's a pretty lass," Mrs. O'Rifcan commented, as she began bustling around the kitchen and grabbing ingredients for what would soon transform into delicious side dishes to go along with the freshly caught fish.

"Don't I know it," Riley admitted. "Bewitched me from the start. That's the unnerving part."

Claron chuckled. "I understand your plight, brother. The best advice I can give you is not to fight it." He grinned as he heard Rhea coming down the back stairwell. She walked up behind him and slipped her arms around his shoulders and hugged him. "Look who decided to show up." She kissed the top of his head before rounding the counter and washing her hands, waiting expectantly for Sidna's directions.

"I hear you are a professional angler," Claron proudly stated.

Rhea laughed. "There's really not much competition." She nodded towards Riley and he squinted in mock disapproval at her statement.

"Heidi be almost ready?" Riley countered.

"Yes." Rhea's smile held a softness to it and she reached across the counter and squeezed his hand. "I love you, Riley O'Rifcan."

Claron's brows rose and Riley chuckled. Before he could think of a joke to rub in Claron's face, Rhea continued. "But if you hurt Heidi, I will sic your brothers on you. You hear me?"

Riley's face sobered a moment and he held up his hands. "You have me word, love. I would never wish to disappoint you, Rhea darling. Especially since you *love* me." He elbowed Claron. "Jealous, brother?"

Claron silently took a sip of his water, his eyes catching Rhea's across the counter, a glint of amusement hidden in the green depths. "Now you've gone and done it, Rhea. You officially made Riley's ego grow beyond the unthinkable."

She laughed as Mrs. O'Rifcan slid a mixing bowl in front of her, Rhea immediately picking up the spoon and stirring.

"It's hard not to have an ego when a lass such as Rhea *loves* me." Riley shoved Claron's shoulder and stood as footsteps could be heard coming down the stairs.

"Don't get too cocky, Riley," Rhea tossed out. "I may love you, but I'm *in* love with Claron. There's a difference."

All teasing slipped from everyone's faces as her words sunk in. She continued stirring, looking down at the bowl, not realizing her slip up. Slowly, her hands stopped, and she gasped as she looked up. "Did I just—"

Mrs. O'Rifcan threw her arms up in the air and hooted, pulling Rhea into one of her bone crushing hugs. Claron stood, his handsome face serious as he rounded the counter. He could feel Rhea's nerves as he reached for her hands and her face flushed scarlet. He lifted her chin and kissed her sweetly on the lips. "And I, lass, am deeply in love with you too."

A quick flash of relief sparked in Rhea's eyes before they began brimming with tears. Claron lifted her off her feet and hugged her until she squealed. The kitchen door opened, and several heads popped inside. "What be the ruckus, Sidna love?" Senior's voice boomed above the cheer.

"Rhea loves me!" Claron yelled, beaming as he squeezed her to his side and kissed her soundly in front of his family.

"Well, blast, Clary, we all know that. I thought something be wrong in here." His simple statement did not deter Senior from slapping Claron on the back in congratulations as he also bent to kiss Rhea's cheek.

Roland stood to the side, his smile content as he clapped his hands and the O'Rifcans celebrated over his granddaughter and Claron.

Riley twirled Rhea in a circle before hugging her close and then his eyes settled upon Heidi at the foot of the stairs. Rhea looked up at him and grinned as she spotted her friend. Slipping from Riley's grasp, Rhea ducked back towards an elated Claron as Riley stepped towards Heidi.

She wore a simple black dress that bared her shoulders, her hair twisted into a tidy French twist minus a few strands that framed her face. Her elegant neck was bare, but she wore delicate dangling earrings that sparkled at her ears. The kitchen fell silent, but Riley heard his heart pounding and could swear it echoed throughout the entire room. "Breathtaking," he heard his Mam murmur to his father, and Riley's heart mirrored the sentiment. Heidi glanced nervously towards Rhea.

Rhea elbowed Claron to help break the awkward moment of silence. He cleared his throat and held a finger up and pointed at Rhea next to him. "Ah... she loves me."

A burst of laughter escaped Rhea's lips as she draped her arm through his and had the entire room erupting in laughter. "Smooth," Rhea whispered to him. "Real smooth."

"It worked, did it not?" He squeezed her side.

Heidi stepped towards Riley's outstretched hand. "Let's escape this madhouse, lass. What say you?"

Heidi grinned. "That sounds perfect."

"Clary," Riley called at the door. "Rhea." He bounced his eyes between the two. "I'm proud of the both of ya. Night to all." He waved at his family as he stepped outside the door to a breath of fresh air and a gorgeous Heidi.

«CHAPTER NINE»

Heidi inhaled a deep breath as they stepped out into the empty café's seating area and walked across the patio towards the street. Chloe, Murphy, and Tommy stood beside a long table, the stench of fish surrounding them. A plop sounded and Chloe huffed. "If the two of you don't stop acting the maggot, I'll be turnin' the hose on the both of you." She glanced up at the sound of heels on stone and did a double take of Heidi before she smiled in welcome. "And where the two of you be off to?" She swiped the back of her hand over her forehead to tidy the loose curl that slipped from her hair tie and then, realizing she'd just spread fish guts in her hair, she held her hand before her and gagged.

Riley chuckled as he gently placed a hand on Heidi's back. "I'm whisking our Heidi off to Galway for a meal."

Murphy turned and his eyes danced as he surveyed Heidi. He nudged Tommy to turn around and the other O'Rifcan coppertop cast a glance over his shoulder. Liking what he saw, he turned as well and both brothers leaned against the table with pleased smirks. "Catch you a rustler there, brother?" Murphy asked.

"Aye. The best one, I believe." Riley nudged Heidi to keep walking.

"Stunning, Heidi love," Murphy called after them. "Be a gentleman, brother."

Riley waved away his comment as he opened his truck door for Heidi and she slid inside.

"A sight to be sure." Chloe watched as Riley slightly fumbled his keys and a tender smile tilted her lips. "He's nervous. Don't believe I've ever seen Riley nervous."

Tommy rubbed his bearded chin. "Aye, a rare occurrence. But when a lass looks like that, any man would be a jumble of nerves."

"I believe her vision will haunt me the rest of the night." Murphy turned back to the fish and snickered at the unamused Chloe as she did the same.

"Think he'll fall for her?" Chloe asked, her tone serious. She looked to her two older brothers as they pondered the question.

"If it be anybody, it would be Heidi," Murphy commented.

"And why do you think that?" Curious, she waited to hear Murphy's logic.

"She's a tough one. A go-getter. She's been plain enough that she has a glad eye for Riley. She be determined, and what man could stand against that?" He motioned towards the truck as it pulled away.

"True. She did look gorgeous in that dress," Chloe added.

"Might be an understatement. Looked dainty as a fairy, that one." Tommy tossed a sliver of fish into a bowl of water and continued running his knife under the scales of the next one.

"Next we know, you two will be traipsing after American women with your tongues to the floor. Seems to be a trend as of late."

Murphy guffawed. "That be the day. I tell you now, little sister, I have no plans to be wooed. 'Tis not in me cards."

"And I already have me eye on someone," Tommy admitted, catching his siblings by surprise.

"And who might that be?" Chloe asked, charmed that her brother would admit to such a thing.

"Denise O'Malley."

"Tom O'Malley's daughter?" Murphy and Chloe inquired at the same moment.

"That be the one."

"And have you taken the lass out?"

"A few times, yes." Tommy ignored their stares and kept working, his large hands moving swiftly from fish to fish.

"I was just meeting with Tom today about the flower festival," Chloe stated. "And he didn't say a word about this. And Tom would, no doubt."

"If he knew," Murphy concluded, eyeing his brother. A cunning grin split his face. "You sly dog!" He punched Tommy. "O'Malley has no clue you be eying Denise, hmm?"

"Not yet, no. And it best stay that way or I know who to pummel."

"But why not tell him?" Chloe asked. "He be kind."

"Aye. But he's nosier than our Riley. Denise and I would have zero privacy after that. It's still early on, best taking it slow and then we will mention it to 'im."

Chloe sighed as she set her knife down. "I think I will be seeing if Mam needs help with the rest of the food. You two handle the rest?"

"Aye. We can." Murphy accepted the quick kiss to the cheek in thanks as Chloe did the same to Tommy, adding a special squeeze to his shoulder on her way into the kitchen, her heart pleased her brother had found someone special. When she stepped inside, it was mere seconds before an excited Rhea assaulted her with the latest development in her relationship with Claron. Love seemed an epidemic.

∞

He pulled the chair out and waited for Heidi to take a seat. As she did, she gently placed her clutch on the table and allowed him to scoot her closer to her place setting. Before rounding her chair, Riley took a deep breath and ran a hand through his hair. He eased into his chair with a confidence he wasn't quite feeling.

Heidi's eyes bounced from table to bar, curtain to window, waiter to bartender, and everything in between as she surveyed the surrounding scene with her mouth slightly agape. "This is a fancy place." She placed her cloth napkin in her lap.

"Aye." Riley motioned for their attending waiter. "Aunt Grace brought me here last month as a thank you for helping Rhea adjust to Ireland."

Heidi chuckled. "Actually, Aunt Grace brought you here because you are a young handsome man and she wanted a date. Rhea was her excuse."

Riley flushed and shrugged. "You're probably right, but I'd like to think it was her gratitude that won me a free meal."

"Evening," the server handed each of them a black menu and began prattling on about drink specials. Heidi ordered a white wine while he went with a dry red. Darting away to fetch their drinks, Riley leaned forward. "So, Heidi Rustler, tell me... what has been your favorite thing about Ireland so far?"

She perused her menu and glanced over the top. Her right brow slightly rose. "Just one thing?"

"Or more." Riley leaned back against his chair and relaxed as the server delivered their drinks and took their orders.

"Fish?" Riley asked her, when the man walked away.

"Yes, fish. Today's activity sparked my hunger for it. I imagine the fish here is better than the one I caught with my hands."

"I don't know about that. Me Mammy can cook a mean fish." He winked.

"Of that, I have no doubt." Heidi took a sip of her wine. "And that is definitely one of my favorite things about Ireland. Your Mam. She's a fantastic woman and an incredible cook."

Her observation warmed him. "Aye, that she is."

"And of course, seeing Rhea and spending time with her. Seeing her happy and in love with Claron is a highlight," Heidi continued.

"She suits me brother well, that is for certain. No better lass for him than our Rhea."

"And I don't think anyone can come to this country and not fall in love with the scenery. Every village, town, and city have charm and history attached to them, and it's all breathtaking." She took another sip of her wine. "I particularly liked Adare."

"It be one of my favorites as well." Riley listened as she continued on with different aspects of her trip. Dancing at Murphy's Pub, fishing in the river behind the B&B, playing pool with him, and dancing with Conor. Heidi loved it all. Coupled with the dreamy look in her eyes when she spoke of her travels, the particular way the candlelight flickered, casting shadows and highlights across her face and hair had Riley enraptured. He blinked, realizing he was losing it.

"And do you plan to visit again?"

"Of course. If Rhea is here, I will most definitely be back. In fact, I guarantee I will be back this summer or fall."

"That so? And why is that?"

"Because those two lovebirds are going to get hitched before we know it."

Riley laughed. "You think so? Wouldn't that be a bit soon?"

Heidi waved her hand. "Please. By looking at them together, it's not soon enough. They're just torturing one another. Rhea will eventually realize that living in Limerick isn't where she wants to be, so she'll move back to the B&B to be closer to Claron. She'll keep her job in Limerick for a while until she realizes there's work she could be doing in Castlebrook. By the time the wedding comes around, Rhea will be fully immersed in all things Claron O'Rifcan."

"I would bet against you if I thought you were wrong. But seeing how I feel the same about the two of them, I will keep my coin."

"Wise man." Heidi smiled and then straightened as she saw their meals arriving. When her fish was placed in front of her, she inhaled a deep and satisfied breath, her eyes sparkling as she told the server thank you. Riley's steak slid in front of him and he felt his mouth instantly water.

"To friends and family. Sláinte." Riley raised his glass and Heidi tapped hers against it.

"So, when is your last day in Ireland?" Riley asked.

"I fly out, not tomorrow, but next Sunday."

"A week? That's all we have left of you here?" Riley frowned. "That won't do."

"Well, it sort of has to." Heidi laughed. "I need to find a job in Texas. My belongings are still in storage, and unless I want to live in my parents' guest house for the rest of my life, I need to find an apartment. All of that is waiting on me. Sounds fun, doesn't it?"

"Are you happy with your decision to move back to Texas?" he asked.

She nodded. "Yes. I mean, I enjoyed living in Maryland, but it wasn't home."

"I understand that. Being in Galway most of the week makes me appreciate my own home more."

"I appreciate your home too. It's gorgeous."

"Castlebrook home? Or my house home?" Riley asked.

"Both." Heidi grinned as she took another bite of her fish.

"How about a sample, Heidi love?" Riley reached his fork towards her plate and she swatted his hand.

"I don't think so, champ."

Riley's brows rose. "A little stingy, are we?"

"This is incredible. I'm not sharing. But nice try. Order it next time you come with Grace."

Riley burst into laughter and Heidi just continued eating as if she didn't care that people began staring at their table. He liked that. He liked her. And he definitely liked looking at her tonight. He reached across the table and tucked a loose strand of hair behind her ear. Her fork froze halfway to her mouth.

He cleared his throat, dropped his hand, and picked his fork up again stuffing a piece of steak into his mouth to avoid fumbling with what to say. He also lifted his free hand to wave for their check. He was starting to feel a bit smothered, and as he adjusted his collar, he hurried through the rest of his steak and finished off his wine. When the check arrived, Heidi was finished as well.

"Dessert?" The server asked.

Riley shook his head and handed him back the bill.

Heidi stood as Riley did and he lightly guided her out of the restaurant and back onto the street, praying for air, and for his sanity to return. However, the way Heidi tucked beside him felt natural. She felt right. And the light scent of the shampoo she'd used wafted up to him making him completely disgusted with himself, because all he could think about was remembering that smell. Remembering the night. Remembering her. And remembering that he'd never quite felt this way before.

∞

"No dessert?" Heidi asked.

"Aye. There will be." Riley pointed up the street. "I'm taking you to a lovely pub that offers not only a nice pint or two, but an interesting dessert that you cannot leave Galway without trying."

"Ah. You have me intrigued." Heidi slipped her arm through his and kept up with his long stride.

"Those shoes made for walking, lass?" He looked down at her heels.

"I wouldn't have bought them otherwise, why?"

"I was thinking we could take the long route. Amble down shop street a ways, Eyre Square. There be neat sights to see."

"I'm perfectly content with wherever you take me, Riley O'Rifcan. I'm full from a fabulous dinner, and feel I should walk off some of what I ate if I'm expecting to fit any dessert in my tummy."

"Tummy?" Riley chuckled. "Are you a wee baby?"

"What? I can't say 'tummy?'" She shrugged. "Stomach, then."

"You can say what you wish, love. Just pointing out that it was adorable."

"Ah, well that's good." Heidi pointed to a bright red building on the corner. "Oh, wow. Look at that." As they rounded the corner her eyes widened at the entire street. Shop street was a pedestrianized thoroughfare surrounded by lovely brick buildings, brightly colored storefronts, and pubs all boasting about serving the 'best plain in Galway.' Riley steered her towards a green building and opened the door. Music played softly in the background and small tables were scattered around a small stage that currently sat empty save unoccupied instruments with the promise of live entertainment hanging in the air as several couples occupied the tables and waited in anticipation.

Riley walked up to the bar and tapped his knuckles. A blonde head popped up immediately and had both he and Heidi jolting in surprise. Sparkly hazel eyes crinkled at the corners as the barkeep restrained a laugh. "Riley O'Rifcan," she greeted warmly, extending her hand. Riley kissed the back of it.

"Piper."

"And where did you find such a beautiful lass?" She nodded towards Heidi.

"She be a friend of Rhea's."

"Ah, how is Rhea? Married your brother yet?"

"Not yet."

Piper swiped her hand over her forehead sending her bangs in several different directions. She was fit and petite in stature, her broad smile taking up most of her face when she flashed it. She spoke with a softer lilt than Heidi had heard thus far in Galway and wondered where she actually came from originally. She was cute and spritely and judging by the gleam in her eyes, fun. Heidi liked her instantly.

"Well, what can I do you for? Got a mouth on ye? Or a throat?"

"Both." Riley tilted his head as if she should know what he spoke of and Piper snapped her fingers.

"Ah. I have just the thing then. Go grab a table. The band will be back on in a few and I'll bring it over. Nice to meet you, Heidi. And welcome to Galway."

Piper darted away and Riley escorted Heidi to one of the tables tucked against the wall. "She seems great."

"Aye. Piper be a wonderful lass. I bring some of my clients here every now and then and she makes a positive impression for Galway."

"I'm not a client. Why did you bring me here?"

Riley looked up as Piper slid a pint glass to the center of the table and buzzed away.

"What is that?" Heidi's eyes widened and Riley smiled.

"The reason I brought you here, love." Riley handed her a spoon. "This be a Guiness float."

"I've never seen this before. I've had a root beer float, but an actual beer float? Is it good?" Her spoon hovered over the glass.

"Would I have made a special trip here? Would I have ordered it for you to try?" He dipped his spoon into the cup and pulled out a sample and ate it. "See, not disgusting."

Heidi dipped her spoon and hesitantly touched the tip of her tongue against the beer and chocolate ice cream mixture. Surprise registered in her navy eyes and she sampled the entire spoon. "I can't believe it." She took another bite. "It's actually delicious."

"Aye. A dessert that was worth the wait." Riley grinned and slightly turned as the band took to the stage again but then faced Heidi once more.

"Thank you, Riley."

His eyes lit as a kind smile spread over his face. "You're welcome, lass. Thank you for joining me."

They sipped on their float in silence as the band played. When they finished, Riley stood and held out his hand. Heidi took it and relished the feel of his fingers laced with hers. She felt content. Happy. And overly full. But all she could think was how the evening would definitely be one of the top highlights of her trip, and she hated that she would not be able to see Riley once she was back in Texas. But her life was there, and his life was in Ireland. Two separate worlds. As she walked the streets of Galway back towards his vehicle, Heidi absorbed every sight, sound, and scent of the city that she would now forever associate with Riley O'Rifcan.

∞

He drove down a couple of side streets and parked along the footpath in front of a small storefront of painted yellow bricks and a vibrant blue door. The sign on the door bore Riley's architecture firm's emblem and his name. He helped Heidi out of his truck.

"And what's this place?"

He reached into his pocket and pulled out a key and unlocked the door. "My latest project. The one that keeps me in Galway."

"This tiny place is where they want the modern art museum?"

"Tiny?" He tilted his head and grinned as he opened the door.

The front entry was a tightfitting hallway with burgundy walls and mustard trim, the tiles beneath their feet a chessboard pattern.

"Interesting choice," Heidi mumbled.

He laughed. "This is not my design, I assure you." She followed behind him as he walked further down the small hall and towards a set of double doors at the end. "Used to be an old dance hall with a pub at the back. Been closed about three years or so. The location is prime in relation to Eyre Square. And the building itself has a history beyond the last business that was here."

He opened the French doors into a large open room under phase one of demolition. Heidi looked up to a tarped ceiling, one edge pulled back to reveal the night sky blended with Galway's city lights. She looked to Riley.

"You must be really good at your job, because I do not see how this could ever become a museum."

He motioned for her to follow him towards a small room behind the old bar counter. A desk sat with his sketches and Heidi's eyes eagerly roamed over them. "Oh." She ran a hand over the one that offered a glass ceiling. "You and your glass."

He grinned. "I thought about what you said. About the more intimate surroundings being more inviting, and no stark lighting. No better lighting than the sun. And on rainy days, which this is Ireland, there will definitely be rainy days... track lighting along the walls to spotlight the pieces." He walked out and into the grand room. "There be retractable wall inserts and free-standing lights next to each for the center of the room. Very modern. Chic. That way, depending on the mood of the gallery manager or the exhibit, the show floor can be rearranged."

Eagerly, he walked towards the bar again. "Obviously we will be taking this out to create more floor space." He glanced up. "The ceilings be..." he thumbed his fingers in front of himself and counted to himself. "Converting for you, lass..." He tallied his fingers in the air. "Thirty-six feet high, if me calculations are correct for your metrics. Gives the patron an eye-opening vision when they take that first step into the room through the doors." He motioned towards the French doors that led to the main entrance. "We be keeping the original entry, as it dates back to the origins of the building. Though we will most definitely be changing the colors of it." He tucked his hands into his pockets. "Well, what do you think? I know it's a bit hard to look past the rubble at the moment, but there's charm."

Heidi turned in small circles as she studied the walls and ceilings, the hardwood floors beneath her shoes. "I like the idea of the glass roof. With this building nestled between two others, you don't have that natural light filtering in from anywhere, and I think it will be a nice dramatic effect."

"Aye, that's the goal."

"And this is where you plan to turn the doorways into arches?" She motioned towards the door that led to his makeshift office.

"Aye. Widen it, turn it into an actual office, put a small hallway that houses the toilets along the way."

"Smart." Heidi stepped over a broken beam towards the center of the room and stood.

He held up his phone and snapped a quick picture of her. At the sound, she turned. "Did you just take my picture?"

"Guilty." He slipped his phone back into his pocket.

"Why?"

"I liked the look of you standing amidst my work." And it was the truth. He appreciated her attention, and her genuine interest in his vision for the place. And she seemed to understand it and visualize the finished space along the same lines as him. She gushed over some of the intricate wall sconces that he planned to restore to their former glory and marveled at the hideous burgundy walls in the entry, that upon her closer inspection, she realized were velvet. Which then led to her threatening his life if he kept them.

When they stepped back onto the street, she rested her hand on the truck door handle and stared at the building with familiarity. "How long will this project take you?"

He ran a hand over the back of his neck as he studied the building before them. "Depends. We're aiming to finish within a year. There be some foundational issues we have to address before we can really do anything. And I have to try and find the right people for the project."

"I'll be back when it opens."

He eyed her serious face, her eyes holding his. "That be the plan, then."

Smiling, she opened her own door and tucked herself back into his truck. Riley eyed the building one more time before slipping into the driver's seat and heading back towards Castlebrook.

«CHAPTER TEN»

Soft feminine chatter filtered up the stairwell as Heidi paused a moment to guess which O'Rifcan ladies resided in the kitchen before entering. Lorena's gentle directions to her daughter, Emily, blended with Sidna's cheerful tone as she conversed with Rhea. And a brief spat between Layla and Chloe could be heard, Layla once again in a mood no one could decipher. Heidi cleared the landing and all eyes fell upon her.

Rhea spun around on her stool and grinned. "So... how was Galway?"

Heidi trudged towards the bar and sat next to her, Rhea's excitement over the possibility of Heidi and Riley as a couple had Heidi placing a calming hand on her friend's shoulder. "Easy, tiger. Let me have some coffee first."

Laughing, Rhea hopped to her feet. "I'll get it for you so you can start telling us all about your romantic evening with Riley."

Heidi just shook her head in dismay but smiled as all the women stopped what they were doing to gather closer to listen. Lorena even stopped her work at the stove, handing the spoon over to Emily so as not to miss out on the scoop. "Wow," Heidi nervously grinned. "You all really want to know?"

A collective "yes" had her straightening on her stool. "Well..." She took a sip of the coffee Rhea offered her. "It was nice."

"Nice?" Disappointment laced the word as if flew from Chloe's mouth, and she bit back another comment as Sidna shot her a look of warning.

Heidi giggled. "He took me to a fancy restaurant. We talked. Went to a pub and listened to some music, had an amazing dessert, and then he showed me his current job site."

"That's not a romantic evening." Layla, baffled Riley would disappoint her so, just shook her head in pity.

"And did he kiss you?" Rhea asked.

Heidi's cheeks pinked. "No."

"No?!" All the woman gasped.

Heidi couldn't contain herself and neither could the other women at their own resounding response and all started laughing.

Sobering, Heidi held up a hand. "It's for the best though. I leave this weekend. I wasn't looking for a relationship in coming here. I wanted to have an evening with Riley, and I got one. It was pleasant and fun and not at all disappointing."

"You aren't staying here?" Rhea asked.

Heidi looked confused. "Why would I stay here?"

Embarrassed for her wishful thinking, Rhea sighed. "I was just hoping something serious would develop between you and Riley and you would want to stay here."

Heidi shook her head. "I once moved across the country to follow a man, and we both know how that worked out. I was stuck in Maryland for three years before I had the courage to move back to Texas. I'm not chasing a man again. So no, I will not be moving to Ireland just to be with Riley. Besides, we barely know one another. Is he fantastic? Yes. Is there something about him that gets under my skin? Yes. There is something different about him, but I'm chalking that up to him just being a unique guy with a good heart. For me, that's not worth crossing an ocean for. There needs to be more."

"You told me just last night that you felt something more for him," Rhea countered.

Heidi shrugged. "I had time to think about it. I'm not willing to face another Chase scenario, Rhea."

"But it's Riley," Rhea pleaded. "You two have held a spark since you first laid eyes on one another. We all see it."

"And I'm saying that's not enough."

"It could be, if you gave it more time. You were oozing love last night before you left, so what happened?"

"I was not 'oozing' anything." Heidi, starting to tire of the third degree, shifted on her stool and took a sip of her coffee. "You and Claron fell for one another fast, Rhea. I understand that. But that is not how it happens for everyone."

"It could. You're just running scared. I think last night went better than you're letting on and it has you worried that you would *want* to move across the ocean to be with Riley. Because you're scared it would turn out to be like Chase. Even though it won't. Because Riley is *not* Chase."

"Enough." Heidi's tone was sharp as if Rhea had hit too close to home. "It's ridiculous to even think about. I've known him a couple of weeks. It's absurd to think beyond that."

"I only knew Claron a couple weeks and knew I did not want to leave," Rhea added, her tone softening.

"Oh, the O'Rifcan men." Sidna reached for a bowl and began her mixing again. "Did you know that Senior and I were married within a week of meeting?"

Rhea and Heidi both gawked at that, and the O'Rifcan sisters smiled.

"A week?" Rhea and Heidi asked in unison.

"Everyone's told me you two fell fast for one another, but a *week*?" Rhea just shook her head. "That's hard to even fathom."

"Oh, don't I know it." Sidna chuckled. "The cheeky boyo had me tied up in knots so. That charming smile he has, oh, he used it as a weapon. And it worked. Charmed the socks right off me." She paused in her stirring and stared off a moment as if remembering, her smile tender. "Senior was a handsome lad, still is. But it was the connection we had. Met him on the cliffs at Angel's Gap. Clary's place. Though then, it belonged to Senior's parents. I was there, sent by me own parents to deliver a blanket to Aibreann, his mother. My mam had made it for her— sold them she did— and Aibreann had purchased this particular one. Well, off I went. Came to Castlebrook from Limerick to obey me mam's bidding and as I knocked on the cottage door, a man rounded the corner of the house. Tall, handsome, a smirk on his face. I was lost." She began stirring again. "Scared the bejesus out of me at the time. Stealthy, he was. Told me his mam had gone to fetch the messages and wasn't home."

"And then what happened?" Rhea rested her chin in her hands, and glanced briefly at Heidi who did the same, both eager to listen to more.

"Oh, he was right charming. Told me, as I was there and he needed help, to set that blanket down and follow him." She chuckled. "Blinded by that gorgeous face, I foolishly complied, only to find meself elbow deep in cow dung and me new dress ruined by the end of it. But I helped him milk the cows. Complete disaster it was. But we laughed together. That's the important part of it all. To laugh. Your partner needs to bring you joy. If you don't feel that when you are with them, 'tis not the right man." She eyed all the women in the room with her words.

"So what made you go from milking his cows to marrying him?" Heidi asked. "In a week?"

"Well, by the time his da and mam came home, we were on the porch sitting and talking of our lives. I was not accustomed to Castlebrook. Though it be a nice village now, it was nothing but a couple of buildings back in those days. I was from the city. I enjoyed my buildings and shopping. But he made life in Castlebrook sound exciting, and I suppose it has been, with him. He decided he liked the look of me." She laughed. "Told me so too. Bold and blunt as he is today, the fool." She handed the bowl to Lorena and her daughter began filling muffin tins as her mother continued. "I happened to like the look of him as well. I went home, and a few days later he turns up at me door with a bouquet of flowers he'd picked and brought straight from his farm. Told me he'd been thinking of me ever since. Told me da that he'd picked me out and settled on me for his wife. That he could wait as long as necessary for me hand, but that it would suit him just fine if he didn't have to."

"Wow." Rhea beamed, and Heidi lightly squeezed her friend's shoulder knowing Rhea's heart for Claron Junior echoed the same sentiments.

"Oh my heart melted at that. And though it was scary, I knew he was indeed the one for me as well. So, me da turned to me and said, "Sidna, what say you of this lad here?"

"So, I looked in Claron's eyes and said, "He'll do, Da. He'll do me just fine." And that was that."

Sighing, Rhea reached across the counter and squeezed Sidna's hand. "I think I'm in love with him now too."

Guffawing, Sidna patted her hand. "The charm he has passed down to each of his own sons. Those devious lads. Charm is part of who they are, down to their bones."

Chloe nudged Rhea's shoulder. "Seems Clary and Rhea are well on their way to follow your steps Mam. Though it not be a week."

"It would have been if I had my say," Rhea admitted and had all the women laughing.

Heidi sat, unsure what to make of Sidna's history. Yes, it was remarkable, but life and love did not happen like that anymore. You didn't know a person after just a week. "How was it marrying a man you didn't know that well?"

"Oh, we had our troubles here and there. Mostly stubbornness, the two of us, butting heads and all. But you grow together. Learn. Accommodate. Compromise. I found my time with him was more important than my desires to live in the city. And we had children right off. Lorena came quickly and brought us closer together. 'Tis wonderful to have a wee baby around the house. Brings a new side to each of you that makes you love one another deeper than before." Sidna gently brushed a hand over Lorena's hair and cupped her cheek. Lorena smiling at her mother. "Little did we know we would end up with an entire brood of little ones. But it was how we wanted it. We loved having a family, a large one at that. There's never been a dull day."

"That is so beautiful." Rhea leaned back in her chair and studied Heidi.

"I need to find a man like Da," Chloe said. "A man that will take one look at me and then sweep me off my feet. Wouldn't that make the dating game much easier?"

"Love at first sight is rare," Layla interjected. "Sometimes you have to try a little bit of everything until you know what you want."

"Love and fate have their own ways," Sidna added. "You will all find it in your own time. No need to rush. I have learned that it tends to find you when you least expect it."

"It surprised me, that's for sure." Rhea's eyes sparkled. "And now I can't imagine life without Claron."

"Then why are you still living in Limerick?" Layla asked.

"I'm not in any hurry. I like where we are at right now. Plus, it helps being in Limerick for my new job."

"You should just keep books for Claron," Heidi suggested. "He needs help, right? And you're the perfect person to do it."

"He has yet to ask me," Rhea pointed out. "And until that day, then I'm content where I'm at."

"I'd hire you to do mine as well," Chloe said. "I hate numbers."

Heidi held up her hands. "See, Rhea. You've already got two clients. Boom."

Sidna chuckled. "'Tis fine to wait, dear." She squeezed Rhea's hand. "The day will come and when it does, it will be grand."

"Exactly," Rhea agreed. "And besides, we aren't supposed to be talking about me. We were talking about you." She pointed to Heidi.

"I expect to fly out on Sunday as planned."

Disappointment settled among the women. "I'll be back though. I promised Riley I would come for the opening of the art museum."

"That could be forever," Rhea whined.

"Or your wedding... if that is sooner." Heidi playfully punched Rhea's shoulder.

"Speaking of weddings," Chloe wiped her hands on a towel. "I have to go to me shop and work on sample arrangements for a wedding I have scheduled for the summer, to give the bride options to look at. Heidi, you still wish to help me with flower festival preparations?"

"Yep." Heidi stood.

"Good. Come along, I'll steal you away from all this love talk."

"You're a saint." Heidi beamed as she slipped off her stool and walked her mug to the sink.

"I'll swing by at lunch and bring you girls some grub," Rhea called. "And maybe I could help with some flowers while I'm at it."

"Do you not have work today?" Heidi asked.

Rhea glanced at her watch and her eyes widened. "Oh my, it's Monday!" She jumped to her feet. "I keep thinking it's Sunday. Oh no..." She rushed towards the door and grabbed her purse. "Delaney is going to kill me." She held a palm to her forehead. "Give me your work number, Rhea," Layla told her. Without thinking, Rhea rattled off the telephone number as she grabbed her keys and draped her purse over her head and across her body. "See you guys this evening." She darted out the door.

Layla reached for the phone and dialed. "Hello. This be Layla O'Rifcan calling on behalf of Rhea

Conners." She paused a moment. "Yes, may I please speak to a Mr. Delaney? Oh, thank you."

"What are you doing?" Chloe whispered, eyes wide.

A deep voice echoed over the phone. "Ah, Mr. Delaney, is it?" Layla asked. "Ah, good. My name is Layla, I be Rhea Conners' friend... oh yes, I know she has not made it in just yet this morning. I'm afraid I had her a bit detained. Women talk and all." She smirked to the women around her. "So understanding of you Mr. Delaney. I apologize again for keeping her from her work. It won't happen again. Oh, and Mr. Delaney?" Layla continued. "Could you please not let on to Rhea that I called. Mortified, she'd be at such a thing. Wanting to make a good impression and all." Her voice dripped honey as she smiled. "Thanks a portion. Have a care." She hung up. "Done."

"What did you just do?" Chloe asked.

"Seems Rhea's boss is very understanding of 'women talk'..."

"Layla..." Sidna warned.

"'Twas not a lie. Men just grow uncomfortable at the thought of what we women would discuss in private. He asked nothing, only said he understood, and that he would not bring it up to

Rhea. And now she can be a few minutes late and her boss will not be angry with her."

Shaking her head, Chloe walked towards the door with Heidi. "Well, Layla has apparently saved the morning. Perhaps Heidi here can save the afternoon by helping me with me flowers." Chloe grabbed her keys. "See you all at the meal."

Heidi waved as she and Chloe hurried towards the small compact car parked along the curb and Chloe hopped inside. Surveying the B&B, Heidi smiled to herself. Rhea's future family was amazing. Yes, the O'Rifcan men may be charming, but the women in the family certainly gave them run for their money. That thought warmed her as she thought about Rhea speeding to work expecting an angry boss and only discovering placidity, and all because of Layla O'Rifcan's charm.

«CHAPTER ELEVEN»

"I'm still unsure about this." Claron rubbed a hand over his lightly bearded jaw as Riley wisped his pencil over the graphing paper and elongated the kitchen bar.

"Trust me." Riley pointed to it. "How's that?"

"'Tis a bit better, I guess." Claron eased into his chair and watched as Riley continued sketching. "You sure you have time for this today, brother? Should you not be in Galway working?"

"Galway is underway. Much accomplished yesterday."

"And how be your night with Heidi?" Claron asked.

"Grand," Riley replied, not looking up.

"That's it?" Claron questioned.

Riley's blue eyes darted to his brother's. Sighing, Riley tossed his pencil down. "She's a fine lass, our Heidi. I enjoyed every second with her. Is that better?"

Claron shrugged. "Was just curious. You've been quiet, and normally when you take a lass out I hear more details than I care to."

"Not much to say. It was a brilliant night. She's great company."

"And?" Claron asked.

"And what?"

Claron smirked.

"That would be a no." Riley pointed to his brother's face and Claron laughed.

"You didn't kiss the woman? Now that *is* a bit odd for Riley O'Rifcan."

"What would be the point of kissing her? She leaves at week's end."

"Ah, there it is." Claron leaned back in his chair and took a sip of his lemonade, Holstein, his cat, jumping onto his lap and rubbing his head on the bottom of Claron's glass. Claron swatted the cat away. Holstein took no offense and weaved around his owner's legs and purred.

"I thought about it," Riley admitted. "A great deal, actually. But it wouldn't be fair. To either of us."

"And why is that?"

"Because she's leaving."

"That hasn't stopped you before. There be plenty of women you've kissed and they departed somewhere."

"This is different. Heidi is different," Riley grumbled as he pulled out a different sketch and slid it before Claron. "Here's my second thought for the upstairs addition."

Claron leaned forward and studied the drawings. "I like this one best. Blends better with what is already here."

"Aye, my thoughts as well."

"And how is Heidi different?"

Riley growled. "Clary, can we just work on your house plans? I came here to escape Murphy's inquisition. I do not want yours."

"Alright." Claron shifted in his chair and gave the drafts more of his attention.

"She just has a way about her," Riley interrupted.

Claron peered up over his glasses. "This be Heidi then?"

Frustrated, Riley stood and walked over the refrigerator and pulled out the pitcher of lemonade and refilled his glass. "Aye, who else would I be talking about? You just asked me about her."

"Thought you didn't want to discuss her. My mistake." Claron's lips quirked as he watched his flustered brother take a long gulp of his drink and storm back to the table and sit.

"She drives me mad." Riley raked a hand through his hair. "Bloody mad."

"How so?"

"For starters, she shows up here and decides she likes the look of me and keeps nagging me about it until I bloody like the look of her."

"Pretty sure you liked the look of her from the start, brother. I was there."

"Eejit," Riley murmured before continuing. "I just meant that she flaunted herself in front of me and made me wish to know her more, and then last night we have a grand time, which only makes me wish to have more time with her... but she plans to leave this weekend. Head back to Texas."

"And?"

"And? *And?*" Baffled, Riley threw his hands up in the air as if Claron were a simpleton. "She led me on."

Claron tilted his head at that observation. "Did she now?"

"Aye. Telling me she wanted me to take her out and all. And then when I do..." Riley exhaled a deep breath. "She bloody ruined me, brother. I— look." Riley scrolled through his phone and pulled up the photo from Heidi standing in the middle of his work site.

"She looks lovely," Claron complimented.

"Lovely? She looks perfect." Riley tossed his phone on his table. "I've caught meself staring at it several times today... like a loon. I've never shown a work project to a woman I was dating, much less one I take out to dinner *once*. She's completely ruined me, brother. Messed everything up."

"And what exactly is she messing up, Riley? Seems to me you're just interested in her and that's not a bad thing."

"She's leaving, Clary. And what am I to do when she leaves?"

Claron shrugged, not sure how to respond. Seeing Riley torn up over Heidi was surprising. His brother was the carefree and flirty type of guy.

Never settle down, always up for a good time. No commitment. And yet, here he sat, driven crazy by a bold woman from Texas who'd taken his brother's heart and punched some life into it. Claron was more impressed with Heidi by the second, though he did feel some sympathy for Riley as well. Despite the fact that he found his brother's current state slightly humorous, he also understood the feelings Riley currently fought. He'd battled his own feelings towards Rhea in the beginning, but he found that when he finally recognized that his life was better with her and that he would do anything to make that happen, his life and heart had been happier than ever. Riley was still in the acknowledgment phase. He smirked at that. Once his brother realized his feelings for Heidi were real and worth his full effort, he'd be able to accept the changes it would bring to his life. One thing was for certain though. His brother was in love with Heidi Rustler, or well on his way, and he'd be a fool to let her go.

∞

The Flower Festival. Had Heidi known what she was signing up for when she agreed to help Chloe, she may have run in the opposite direction as fast as possible. Instead, she had naively accepted the role as apprentice and consequently she found herself nursing a sore fingertip in her mouth. Thorns. She never thought about the thorns on roses. When she purchased them back home, she just grabbed them from the store and the thorns had already been trimmed. Now, she understood the work behind the presentation. She'd trimmed so many thorns off roses, her hands looked like pin cushions. Chloe zoomed through bundle after bundle as if she wasn't even aware of the pokey ninjas that struck when you least expected it. But despite the nuisance, Heidi did have to admit that she was having a great time. Layla, Chloe, and Rhea sat at a long table with her and all of them tied small bundles of flowers together. *Bouquets,* she corrected herself.

"And so, I darted to Limerick last night to enjoy a nice meal with Barry," Layla continued.

"Barry?" Heidi listened.

"The man that lives across the courtyard from Rhea. He's a dream, Heidi. Complete dream." Layla then frowned. "But a complete bore."

"Layla," Chloe chided.

"What? He was. Trust me, I was just as disappointed."

Rhea grinned. "If you had just asked, I could have told you that."

"Oh, so you know Barry now?" Layla asked.

"We've bumped into one another at the mailboxes and the elevator now and again. He always seems a bit... dull."

"Exactly. Nice man, that Barry, but not much excites him," Layla agreed.

Rhea laughed as she tied off her last bouquet and set it in a glass of water. "What next, Chloe?"

"I have the Gerbers next, Rhea love." Chloe pointed to the vibrant daisies that graced the counter, long thick stems in black plastic vases.

A groan floated through the air and Heidi realized it was her own. All the women looked at her and then laughed.

"Sorry, I didn't realize that was out loud."

"You tired of flowers, Heidi?" Chloe grinned.

"There's so many."

"Aye."

"Tell me again what Flower Festival entails."

"Well, there be a small parade down the street. Floats and such. Mainly for the children to create for their different groups and organizations. Live band plays out front of Murphy's Pub. Food available at every turn."

"So, a typical festival."

"Not so," Chloe amended. "The Flower Festival is somewhat known as the Sweetheart Festival as well. See, it's the time of year when a person can boldly profess their hidden love to another. And by the gift of flowers, considered to be good luck because the fairies live in the flowers... you be handin' your love the best of luck there is. A wonderful gift. And the fairies make the flowers bloom and keep so that your love may be reminded of you every day."

"Really you just receive a lot of flowers and it's fun," Layla summed up.

Rhea and Heidi smiled.

"So secret crushes come to light?" Rhea asked.

"Sometimes," Chloe said. "Then you just have those who wish to dote upon their friends or family. There's a big ceremony at the end of the parade. Petals fall. And that is usually when the exchange of kisses or tokens happens."

"So instead of confetti, it's flower petals?" Rhea asked.

"Mmhmm." Chloe pointed to several large trash bags that sat inside her walk-in cooler. "The children throw them from the highest window of all the buildings to shower them about."

"It sounds beautiful."

"And expensive," Heidi added. "Bet this is the best event all year for you, Chloe."

"I don't do poorly, that is for certain. But due to there being so many people who come to Castlebrook from outlying villages and cities, I am not the only florist to participate. There be some from Limerick and Shannon that aid in the supply. I will have a large tent set up for purchase of flowers, garlands, and crowns." She held up a woven crown of small flowers and placed it upon her head. "The littles always enjoy wandering the streets like fairies, so I sell many of these." She removed it and placed it on the table as she continued to make another. "I will have a larger supply this year, thanks to all your help." She eyed the other women around the table.

"I haven't helped that much," Rhea said. "I've only been able to come after work."

"'Tis more all the same." Chloe nodded towards the Gerber daisies and Heidi stood to fetch a vase as well. "Just trim the stems won't you, Heidi?"

An expert at trimming now, Heidi complied.

"Do women give flowers to men during this festival?" Heidi asked.

"Oh yes." Chloe smiled. "Everyone gives and receives."

"Thinking of giving some flowers to Riley?" Rhea baited.

"Actually, yes. I think he would find it fun." Heidi added. "And I like him, so why not?"

"A perfect reason to give him some," Chloe encouraged.

"I do not give flowers to men," Layla adamantly stated and had Chloe rolling her eyes.

"Layla likes to bask." Chloe dramatically sprawled herself back in her chair and fanned herself. "Oh, so many men in love with me." She imitated Layla's voice. "Oh, more flowers.... For me?"

Layla tossed a stem at her, but the sisters grinned at one another.

"I can't help that I receive a bundle or two."

"Or two?" Chloe laughed. "We might as well give you all we've made so far, sister." She turned towards Rhea and Heidi. "Layla tends to receive a mountain of flowers each year."

"And why shouldn't I?" Layla straightened in her chair. "I'm a young, single lass. Perfect recipient."

"Do you expect Gage to give you flowers?" Rhea asked.

"That would be a no," Layla said. "Unfortunately. Though we did bump into one another at the pub the other night and 'twas not awkward."

"That's good." Rhea nodded in excitement. "The guys do not have to worry about losing another friend then. I'm sure Riley is pleased with that."

"Riley not be pleased with anything since his date with Heidi," Layla mumbled.

"What?" Heidi asked.

"Oh, he's in a fit, he is. Grumbly, miserable, and a complete dread to be around at the moment. You've twisted him up so, Heidi. Thrown him out of circuit." Layla started twitching and had Rhea and Chloe laughing.

"I broke him?" Heidi teased.

"Yes," the three other women said in unison. Heidi's smile slowly faded.

"Well, that was certainly not my intention. We had a great time. Not sure why he would be upset over that."

"'Twas the great time that was the problem," Chloe added. "If you want me honest opinion of it, I think he cares for you Heidi, more than he wishes. 'Tis why he's a mess and moody. His heart is giving him fits."

Heidi rested her chin in her hand on the edge of the table as she leaned forward. "Riley is..." She paused to try and think of the right word to describe him. "Breathtaking."

"Oh aye." Layla looked heavenward. "Please do not tell him that. His ego..." She spread her hands around her head as if it grew another ten inches.

Heidi laughed. "It's the only word I can think of. He's a whirlwind. In a good way. Charming, handsome, fun. But when you catch a glimpse of what's underneath all that it steals your breath. And you're caught in that split second of decision: do I fall for him or do I run? Because either way, Riley O'Rifcan is a man that could easily change a woman's life if you let him. He's an all-inclusive man. There is no 'date for a good time.' There is 'fall in love with him completely' or 'run as far away as possible.'"

"And you're choosing to run?" Rhea asked, already knowing the answer.

"Yes," Heidi admitted unashamedly. "I am not ready for something serious. I'm also not ready to fall head over heels for a guy I barely know. I recognize the warning signs, so I'm leaving before I can't escape."

"Doesn't seem quite fair," Rhea added.

"Why?"

"Because he obviously cares for you too. Seems silly for you two not to explore it. What if it could be more?"

"Neither of us are looking for more right now, Rhea," Heidi explained.

"Obviously." Rhea's annoyance dripped from the word and had the O'Rifcan sisters exchanging a quick nervous look with one another.

"Don't get upset with me because you want me to stay here and I'm not," Heidi pointed out.

"It has nothing to do with me," Rhea countered.

"Exactly," Heidi added.

"I just don't like seeing two people I love and care about torture themselves over one another. When, if they would both just suck up their own pride and stupid stubbornness, they could actually be happy. Together."

"Time will tell," Heidi amended. "I plan to visit again at some point."

"And what if you arrive next time and Riley is married to a wonderful woman and starting a family. What then?" Rhea asked. "Will you regret leaving now? Will it devastate you? Will you care?"

"Rhea," Heidi reached over and squeezed her friend's hand. "If Riley finds someone, I would be happy for him. Do I care for him? Yes. But I am not moving across the world to be with him, because I'm not in love with him. It's that simple. If I loved him, then sure, I would stay. But I don't."

"And I don't believe you," Rhea added.

Heidi shrugged and released her friend's hand. "It is what it is."

A chime filtered through the air as the glass entry opened and Conor McCarthy walked inside. "Aye, there be a pretty sight." He beamed as he waved to all the women.

"Conor," Chloe greeted. "What can I do for you?"

"Oh, Chloe, I'm a great fool, I am."

"That is an understatement," Layla teased and received a harsh glare from Chloe before she focused upon Conor once more.

"What is it, Conor?" Chloe asked.

"It be my mam's birthday today, and I've been so wrapped up in helping Riley and Clary at the cott—" he trailed off when he realized Rhea sat at the table. "Helping others with some... things, that

I completely forgot. Do you have some flowers I can take to her? Perhaps she won't think I've forgotten after all."

"Of course. I'll make your mam something special, with her favorites. You can pick them up on your way home this afternoon."

"That'd be right grand, Chloe. Always good in a pinch, you are." He looked at the flowers and leaves scattered about the room. "Flower Festival underway, I see."

"'Tis."

"Looks like you rounded up the prettiest help in County Clare."

Chloe smiled as she walked him towards the door. "Pretty lasses make pretty flowers."

"Aye, I can see that. G'day to you all." He waved as he walked out, and in typical Conor fashion, left the mood brighter than it was before his arrival.

«CHAPTER TWELVE»

The weather was beautiful. The previous night's rain had dampened the earth just enough so that the dust settled and the temperature stayed comfortable, which Riley felt was perfect for a festival day. He strolled up the footpath, hands in his pockets, as he made his way to Murphy's Pub. Decorations were being hung from business storefronts and light posts along the street were draped with hanging baskets of overflowing flowers or garlands. Friendly faces decorated their lots with fresh potted blooms to add even more color to the street's festivities. As he walked up to Murphy's he spotted Piper balancing on top of a ladder, draping a garland full of plump roses around the door frame of the main entrance.

"Top of the mornin' to ye, Piper," Riley greeted. "What brings you all the way down to Castlebrook? A bit far from Galway."

The blonde hair swished as she turned, and she grinned. "Well, well, well. Morning, Riley O'Rifcan. Turns out we know the same people." She pointed to Murphy as he opened the door and almost ran into the ladder Piper staggered upon.

"You know Murphy?"

"Recent acquaintance," Piper said. "Came down this week with some friends and visited the pub."

Murphy grinned. "She's fine help, your Piper, brother," Murphy acknowledged. "I'm trying to convince her to work for me instead of that fancy pub in Galway."

"Good luck," Riley challenged.

"Oh, I believe I'm wearin' on her. 'Tis my untamable charm that's doing the trick." Murphy winked as Piper just shook her head.

"Truth is, I come to Flower Festival every year. Have been since I was a wee lass," Piper explained. "Came late last night to the pub, and Murphy mentioned he needed a hand in decorating the place for the festivities, so I offered. Your Mam supplied me a place to stay and your brother's lass— Rhea, I believe was her name— welcomed me friendly enough."

"A sweetheart, our Rhea."

"She is," Piper agreed. "Heard your sweetheart was to be staying at the B&B as well, but I did not see her last night."

"Hm." Riley ignored the looks of Murphy and Piper as he surveyed their work. "'Tis coming together. Better job than Murphy could have handled on his own. A fine lass you are, Piper."

"'Tis fun to lend a hand."

"Especially to one so handsome," Murphy teased as he walked from one end of the overhanging porch canopy to move an oversized planter exploding with fresh blooms. He slapped Riley on the shoulder as he passed, jostling the planter. Riley reached out and helped him set it down before Murphy lost control and dropped it. "Clary heading up?"

"Aye," Riley stated. "Plans to meet up with Roland and Rhea at Chloe's before the festivities begin. Rhea is helping with finishing projects. As are Heidi and Layla."

"Handy helper, your Rustler."

"She is not mine." Riley plucked a loose petal from the garland and rubbed it between his fingers.

"Is that why you're frownin'?" Murphy asked, looking to Piper as she began bringing out another string of garland from the pub.

"I am not frowning. Just... brooding."

"Ah. Best brood elsewhere then. Only cheerful people allowed in front of the pub. Brooding be bad for business and all. You understand." Murphy waved him away with a teasing glint in his eye.

"Have a care, Murphy. I'll expect a fresh pint later."

"And you shall have it. Piper has offered to lend a hand behind the kegs tonight." Murphy shot a quick glance towards his new helper. "Winning her over already."

Piper snickered behind him as she walked up and draped her elbow on Murphy's shoulder. "Is arrogance a family trait?"

"Yes," both men replied and had her laughing.

"See you two later." Riley slipped his hands back into his pockets and continued to meander up the footpath towards his sister's flower shop. He spotted Conor stepping out and shutting the door behind him.

"Mornin' to ye, Riley." He pumped Riley's hand with vigor as he nodded over his shoulder. "A fine place to be today, so many pretties in there."

"I imagine so."

Conor chuckled. "You planning on handing out some petals today?"

"A few."

"Only a few?" Conor looked baffled. "Riley O'Rifcan be the flower king in years past."

"Unfortunately, I'm in a bit of a mood this year it seems."

Conor's smile faltered. "Everything alright with you, mate?" He placed a concerned hand on Riley's shoulder and his kind eyes grew serious.

Realizing he'd let slip that he was off his axis, Riley forced a smile. "Right as rain. Just finding it hard to wake this morning, I guess."

"Ah, good." Conor patted his shoulder before stepping in the direction he wished to go. "You had me worried there a moment. 'Tis a happy day today, Riley. No time for moods when there's pretty faces and pretty petals to attend to."

"Right you are, Conor. Right you are." His friend waved and carried on down towards the pub, already heckling Murphy from afar, and Riley turned the knob and stepped through the door into Chloe's.

∞

"Ah, there he is. My favorite brother." Chloe beamed as she pointed to a large crate overflowing with flower bouquets. "Be a gentleman, brother, and help me carry those to my stand outside?"

Heidi looked up and spotted Riley and saw a flash of annoyance cross his face as Chloe immediately put him to work. He turned to greet the remainder of the room and his eyes fell upon her. She now wished she'd freshly combed her hair. Or put on makeup. But Chloe had bustled them out of the B&B bright and early that morning to come help with last minute arrangements. His eyes fell upon her and she fidgeted under his stare. They hadn't spoken since the night of their date. She'd purposely avoided him. It was easier that way. When she would leave tomorrow, it would be easier. But as he started walking her direction, Heidi's heart galloped into a leap and words lodged themselves in her throat. Chloe intercepted, placing the large crate in his arms and patting his cheek. "There's a good lad, Riley. You can come make eyes at Heidi afterward." She turned his shoulders and sent him out the door. "Sorry 'bout that, Heidi, I just need to borrow his muscles a moment."

Heidi shrugged as if she had no care in the world. Rhea's watchful eyes made her nervous that her feelings were carved on her face.

A minute later he was back. But the productive Chloe was already shoving another crate in his arms before he could even clear the threshold.

"'Tis sheer cruelty, forcing him to work when he just wants a look at Heidi," Layla pointed out as her lips quirked towards Heidi's direction.

"Surprised you're even speaking to her now," Chloe quipped. "You out of your mood, sister?"

"What mood?"

Rhea laughed and had Layla glowering at her.

Chloe grinned at Rhea's response.

"Oh alright, so I was a wee bit jealous of all the attention the new lass was getting." She looked to Heidi. "But now that I know you have eyes for me brother, well... we can be friends."

"So kind of you," Rhea replied sarcastically.

Layla shrugged. "Although... if you receive more flowers than me today, I will certainly be a pest."

"As if you haven't been already?" Chloe's eyes rolled heavenward as the front door opened again and Riley stepped in.

"Any more?" he asked.

"That be the last of them for now. Thanks, brother." He accepted her kiss of gratitude as he walked towards the table. He stuffed his hands in his pockets and rocked back and forth on his heels as he watched the women twist wires, fluff leaves and petals, and braid streamers, their hands quick and efficient. Chloe, their master of arms, hopped back into her chair and expertly started the same process, only faster.

"And what brings you by?" Rhea finally asked, looking up with a knowing grin.

He walked towards her and gripped the back of her chair and quickly tipped her backwards. She squealed as she hovered over the floor. Riley bent forward and kissed her on the forehead before pulling her chair quickly back to all fours. "Just needed to see you, Rhea darling."

Breathless, Rhea placed a hand over her heart and shook her head. "Better be thankful Claron didn't see you do that," she teased.

Riley grinned and then leaned on the table next to Heidi. She tilted her cheek towards him and he flashed a quick grin before kissing it in welcome. "You smell lovely," he complimented, as he reached and tucked her hair behind her ear. Her pulse jumped but she remained focused on her project.

"Thank you."

Riley stood back to his normal posture. "Conor was right. I believe this is the prettiest room of the day so far."

"Will be even prettier when it's set back to rights," Chloe stated, her tiredness already seeping through. "But I believe we have enough for the day, in enough time so that we all may have a quick shower and a glamour to ready ourselves for the festival."

"I could go for a hot shower." Rhea lifted the front of her shirt and smelled. "Can't let Claron see me like this."

"Clary's seen you covered in manure, Rhea. I don't think a little sweat is going to turn him away," Layla pointed out and then rolled her eyes as a dreamy smile washed over Rhea's face. "Oh bother, she's completely worthless now, mentioning Clary and all."

Rhea sighed heavily and nodded. "It's a curse, what can I say?"

Riley chuckled. "'Tis good for Clary to have a lovebird."

"And what of you, brother?" Layla asked, darting a glance at Heidi. "You handing out some flowers today?"

"As always," he replied.

"Good."

"Conor has already challenged me. Seems I have a reputation to uphold."

"Get on with ye!" Chloe hooted with laughter. "Though I will say, all your purchases best come from your little sister or I will have your hide, Riley O'Rifcan."

"I'm a loyal customer." He kissed her cheek on his way to the door. "I will see you lovely ladies at the festival, a flower for each of you. I expect a flush in return, or a bit of a kiss." He tapped a finger to his cheek as he winked.

"You are nothing but trouble." Rhea called at him. "Leave, before you have us all melting into a puddle of mush."

Laughing, Riley waved and walked out.

Heidi released a long breath and the other women cast curious glances her way. "What?"

"You barely spoke to him," Rhea pointed out. "What was that about?"

"I spoke to him."

"You said thank you," Rhea admonished. "That was it." She crossed her arms as if she knew what Heidi was up to.

"Which is polite," Heidi countered.

"Yes, but..." Rhea trailed off and just shook her head in disappointment. "Never mind," she mumbled, sticking a stem into her vase with extra force.

"We've been through this, Rhea," Heidi continued. "I leave tomorrow. What would be the point of encouraging anything?"

"I just think... no, I'm not going to say it." Rhea huffed and stood from her seat to carry her finished arrangement towards the current collection crate.

"No. Say it," Heidi invited. "I want to hear why this makes you so upset."

"Me too," Layla murmured to Chloe, receiving an elbow in the ribs in return.

"You've led him on." Rhea turned, her eyes flashing with heat as she eyed her best friend.

"Excuse me?"

"When you first arrived, you made it your mission to seek out Riley. You even told him you wanted him to ask you out. He resisted. Then when you keep pushing, and he finally does..." Rhea held up her hand to calm herself, her voice shaking as her bravery started to falter. "He finally asks you to dinner. He realizes he does care for you and wishes to get to know you better. You two go out and have an amazing time. And now, all of a sudden, you back off. You don't want anything to do with him. You cast your line, hooked the man you were after, and now you just want to toss him back. It's not fair to him, Heidi. Riley is a keeper. He's not just some... fish." Rhea fisted her hands on her hips. "And now, seeing the way he looks at you and the complete disregard you seem to have for him, well... it just makes me furious. And ashamed of you."

Heidi's eyes widened at Rhea's last remark. "I leave tomorrow, Rhea. To me, I am being fair to him. Nothing can come of this. He lives here, I live in Texas. By distancing myself from him, it will make it easier on the both of us when I leave tomorrow. What's the point in pretending there is more between us than there is? Did I have fun with him? Yes. Do I care for him? Yes. But the fact that I will not move here on a whim doesn't change. I'm going home." Heidi stood, and the O'Rifcan sisters' eyes cautiously bounced between the two women. "And I'm sorry you see me as the villain in all this. It was never my intention to hurt you, Riley, or anybody."

"But if you would just give him a chance," Rhea pleaded. "You could stay longer and just see how things go."

"No." Heidi shook her head. "I won't move somewhere because of a man. Not again."

"But what if he's the *right* man?" Rhea asked.

"Then fate will step in at some point, I guess," Heidi added. "But until then, I'm heading home tomorrow. And I would like it if my last day here is not spent squabbling with my best friend."

Sighing, Rhea dropped her fists and walked towards Heidi and hugged her. "I'm sorry. I just love you both so much and want to see you both happy."

"I know." Heidi released her hold. "And Riley is a fantastic man. It's just not the right timing."

"The day I'd see a woman I actually like slipping through me brother's fingers." Chloe shook her head. "Pity."

Heidi offered a sad smile. "Thanks, Chloe."

Layla, looking in the mirror along the wall, fastened a flower crown around her head. "I will admit it has been fun seeing Riley a bit out of sorts. Shame you won't stay, Heidi. Now that I've decided to like you, I think we could be great friends."

Rhea and Chloe just shook their heads in dismay. Layla looked up from her reflection. "What?"

Heidi grinned. "Likewise, Layla. But I will be back before you know it. I told Riley I would return when his current project is completed, or if Claron decides to pop the question to Rhea. Whichever comes first."

"Oh goodness," Rhea's smile softened. "Claron and I are still early on in our relationship. That could be a while. I want you back here sooner."

"Rhea," Heidi placed her hand on her friend's shoulder. "I love you, but sometimes you can just be completely dense."

Chloe and Layla burst into laughter at the shock on Rhea's face.

"Claron is not going to drag his feet much longer, so you better be ready." Heidi grinned as Rhea's cheeks flushed at the possibility and the assurance from the two sisters. "Now," Heidi looked to Chloe. "What's next this morning?"

«CHAPTER THIRTEEN»

"*I don't care what* you boys say, you're my sweethearts and I gladly give you each a rose." Sidna kissed Murphy on the cheek and squeezed him in one of her signature hugs before placing a clipped rose into his shirt pocket. She then wrapped her arms around Riley and did the same. He gently brushed a hand over her hair as she slipped a peach colored rose into his pocket. Murphy whipped out a corsage and slipped it onto her wrist while Riley placed a flower crown upon her head. Pleased with the attention, Sidna clucked from one boy to the next, each son giving her a flowered token. "All of you look so handsome. The lasses beware today." She giggled as Senior draped his arm around her plump waist.

"Come, Sidna love. We've the rounds to make. Boys—" he looked proudly at each of them. "Don't break too many hearts today." He winked as his bolstering laugh carried them out the door.

A loud clap hit Riley's back as Murphy nudged him towards the door, followed by Claron. "Figured you would be with Rhea, brother," Riley commented, surprised at Clary's presence.

Claron shook his head. "'Tis tradition to shower Mam with flowers here at the pub before venturing to the rest of the festival. Rhea is at Chloe's booth helping sell flowers. I plan to stop there next."

"And what have you for Rhea?"

"My heart. Is that not enough?" He chuckled as he reached into a crate by the front door and pulled out a massive bouquet of mixed blooms he'd gathered from around the farm and had Chloe prepare for him.

"Wow." Piper's eyes lit up from behind the bar counter and she walked towards them. "Any woman would love those."

Murphy pulled his hand from behind his back and offered a small bundle of tulips to Piper. Her face blanched a moment before wonder replaced the shock. "For me?"

"Aye. You've helped me a great deal, Piper lass." Murphy winked. "And it be Flower Festival. No lass should start the day without something cheerful."

She accepted them and accepted the hug from Murphy as Riley tucked a small strand of baby's breath behind her ear. She lightly fingered it as Claron handed her a wildflower from his bouquet. She fanned herself. "You O'Rifcan boys better get out of here. A girl could grow accustomed to this." Laughing she shooed them out the door. The remaining brothers followed, Tommy making a beeline towards O'Malley's Market and his current lady. Jaron set off towards Chloe's booth to purchase a couple of bundles to hand out for the day. Jace, already prepared, made sure to hand Piper a rose on his way out the door towards an awaiting group of females up the footpath. Declan, eyes only for his Aine, headed towards one of the food tables his mother sponsored where Aine volunteered for the day.

Riley observed the smiling faces, some familiar and some visitors from surrounding villages and cities, as well as a few tourists that happened to be in the right place at the right time. He loved Flower Festival. Castlebrook's loveliness was amplified by the natural beauty of different blooms covering its nooks and crannies. He heard her laugh before he saw her. And when he saw her, his heart tripped. *Blasted woman*, he thought, but he couldn't tear his eyes away. Heidi stood in a black jumpsuit, her hair wavy and free down her shoulders and back, a flower garland, like a boa, draped over her shoulders and a crown of petals around her head. She looked, he realized, like a fairy queen reigning above her subjects or even Aphrodite, the goddess of love, as she stood on an empty crate holding several bouquets for Chloe. Murphy stood below her, no doubt confessing his love for her, as men lined up to purchase what his sister had to offer.

He watched as Claron snuck inside the booth behind Rhea as she handed a patron his purchase of crowns. When she turned and saw him, her eyes sparkled with delight and instead of reaching for the flowers, she tenderly reached for Clary's face and planted a sweet kiss to his brother's lips. A small spark of envy stung Riley's gut as he watched them eye one another in love; the easy way Rhea accepted the flowers from Clary, and though she'd been surrounded by flowers for the last three days, Rhea still cried and buried her face in Clary's neck as she continued hugging him. *He wanted that*, Riley thought. The love and tenderness. The devoted eyes looking into his. But as his gaze landed on Heidi, the squeeze in his gut only tightened, and he knew he'd never have it with her if she went home to Texas. What was he to do about that? She was to leave the following day and did not seem bothered that she'd never see him again. Or if she did, only on short trips when she came to visit Rhea. And that bothered him. Because he wanted her to feel more towards him than she did. It was exceedingly frustrating. And if he allowed himself to admit it, it hurt.

Rhea caught his attention and waved, her cheerful heart shining through her smile as she pointed to Clary's bouquet in her hands. Riley walked towards her and accepted her hug and the small necklace of braided blooms she draped over his neck. "For my fairy prince." She winked as she kissed his cheek.

"You flatter me, Rhea love." Riley brushed a fingertip over one of the flowers in her hands. "Clary treating you to a lovely petal, I see."

"Aren't they amazing?" She leaned into Claron's side and slid her arm around his waist.

"You did good, brother," Riley complimented. "Making our Rhea fall even more in love with you."

"'Twas my goal," Claron admitted and had Rhea laughing.

"Like he even needed to." Rhea grinned up at Claron and he tapped her nose.

"I have a gift for you, Rhea." Riley reached into his shirt pocket and pulled out a small necklace of silver. "I know it be Clary's place to bejewel you and all, but I asked his special permission to be the one to share this with you. After all, if it weren't for me you might still be wandering the county line in the pouring rain."

Rhea looked from brother to brother as the chain unraveled in Riley's fingers and a single stemmed silver rose charm dropped on the delicate chain. She gasped. "'Tis custom for an O'Rifcan lass to wear a necklace like this on Flower Festival day." Riley draped the necklace around Rhea's neck and clasped it. Rhea fingered the small rose, her eyes glassing as she restrained her tears. "You be one of us, Rhea. We've said from the beginning that what is Roland's, is ours. And now," he nodded towards Claron. "What is Clary's, is most definitely ours. Happy first Flower Festival, love. We love you."

Rhea swiped away her tears as she wrapped her arms around Riley in a tight hug. "It's so beautiful," she murmured, as she sniffled and pulled away to embrace Claron. "I love you all too." She noticed Chloe and Layla looking her way as they pointed to their own special necklaces. Rhea wiped her cheeks again and shook her head. "I'm not supposed to cry today, Riley. My makeup is going to ruin."

"I'm sure Clary will forgive me this once, and I doubt he will even notice." Riley squeezed her hand. "Enjoy your day, love."

He heard her quiet conversation with Claron, thanking him for loving her, and again, Riley wished those words were for him, only from the woman standing on the empty crate. It was a new and uninvited feeling that he felt had already complicated his life. Heidi stepped down and reached on the table for a bright orange Gerber daisy. "I have been waiting to give this to you." She smiled in welcome as she reached up and tucked the ostentatious bloom behind his ear.

"Am I to seriously wear it like this?" he asked, his nerves coming through as he smiled.

"No. I just wanted to see how it looked next to your black hair." She grinned as she removed it and placed it inside his shirt pocket next to the rose from his mother. Her hand lingered on his chest a moment as she looked up at him. "You okay?"

Nodding, he accepted the bouquet he'd specifically asked Chloe to create for Heidi. A vibrant and cheerful daffodil, hyacinth, and tulip bouquet of oranges, purples, and yellows to match Heidi's bold personality. "I have these for you."

Heidi's brows lifted. "Wow." She accepted them. "I saw these earlier and wondered who the lucky lady would be to receive such a bundle. Thank you."

"Are all the lads showering you with petals, petal?"

Heidi snickered. "That would be a no. And I'm glad, otherwise Layla would not be my friend."

He laughed.

"'Tis true," Layla called from the other side of the booth as she popped a piece of cotton candy in her mouth and grinned at Heidi.

"We've been over it," Heidi told him.

"Care for an amble up the footpath?" Riley nodded in the direction of the sidewalk.

"Sure." She linked her arm with his and rested her bouquet in the crook of her other arm. "Is it wrong of me to carry these to gloat?"

"Not a'tall. I'm standing a bit taller meself with you on me arm." He winked at her as she chuckled.

"It's a beautiful and glorious day today." She sighed and inhaled a deep breath of sunshine and flowers. "I think I will come back for this every year."

"That'd be quite a commitment as I'm sure Chloe would enlist you to help her every year."

"I would be okay with that." Heidi beamed as she pointed to Lorena's youngest, Rose, receiving a crumpled up flower from a small boy.

"'Tis a chance for the lads to be brave, no matter the age," Riley admitted.

"It's cute. And then there's that." She pointed to the food table where Sidna and Claron Senior were wrapped in each other's arms and kissing quite passionately.

"And that," he acknowledged. "Be why there's ten of us children."

Heidi laughed.

A young girl ran up to them and smiled a gap-toothed grin as she held a partially wilted daisy up to Riley. He knelt before her and took her free hand, kissing the back of it as he accepted her gift. He then plucked the rose from his mother out of his pocket and handed it to her. The girl's eyes widened at the beautiful flower and she ran away on a giggle.

"Heartbreaker," Heidi teased.

"Lasses of all ages tend to dote upon me during Flower Festival."

"Is that so?"

He nodded. "Aye. But I am not the only male receiving such attention." He pointed and they watched as several children surrounded Conor McCarthy. Conor made an extravagant show of magics, pulling flowers from behind ears, from his sleeves, and from behind his back to give to all the excited kids. He waved in their direction as he spotted them and with regretful chorus the kids accepted his farewell as he trudged over towards Riley and Heidi.

"Day to ya, Heidi." He reached a hand beside her ear and snapped, a rose emerging in his hand to give to her. She laughed and accepted it with a kiss to his cheek.

"And for you." She handed him a tulip from her bouquet.

"Well now," Conor puffed out his chest and slid the tulip into his shirt pocket. "I'm the proudest peacock here today to be wearin' a flower from such a beauty."

"Easy now," Riley warned playfully.

Conor guffawed in laughter and slapped a friendly palm on Riley's shoulder. "I'm sure I'll see the two of you here and abouts. But I've got me eye on helpin' me Mam for a bit at the tables. Have fun on behalf of me?"

"That we will," Riley agreed. "Careful now, Conor." Conor eyed him curiously. "The little ones do not count towards our flower competition."

Conor's face split into an enormous grin as he laughed. "That be the way of it then. Loser buys the first round at Murphy's."

"A deal's a deal." Riley saluted to his friend as Conor hurried towards his mother's table to help sell snacks to the ever-growing crowd.

"I'll miss him." Heidi studied Conor as he bent down to help his Mam lift a heavy box onto the table.

"Conor is a staple here in Castlebrook. His family all be kind."

"And your family too." She looked up at him. "I'll miss all of you as well."

"Will you now?" He quirked a brow at her and noticed a sudden sadness filter through her gaze before she looked away.

"I've loved my stay here. Hard to believe I head back to Texas tomorrow. The trip has passed quickly."

"I will admit I am not ready for you to leave."

She rested her head against his shoulder. "I'll be back one of these days."

"One of these days," he murmured as he kissed the top of her hair. "Seems a bit long to me."

Heidi lifted her head and looked up at him again, her chin resting on his shoulder. "It's the best I can offer."

Riley's gaze hardened a moment until he looked away and began leading her back towards Chloe's booth. "Best get you back, lass. I'd hate for Chloe to think I've stolen her help." He calmed his irritation by releasing his hold on Heidi and hurrying towards his mother's table. He'd spend most of his day helping Lorena and Mam and then perhaps the bitterness that had started to settle in his chest would ease. But when he looked at Heidi all he felt was a sense of longing, followed by frustration. The woman was eating him alive and spitting out his core, and there was nothing he could do to stop her. And he hated the feeling.

∞

Heidi handed a bundle of roses to an elderly man, his small hat clenched in nervous fists as he took them and slowly made his way towards a woman around his age. She sat in a wheelchair, her hair perfectly tied back into a bun. Her face was thin, and her lips painted a bright red, but when she spotted the man, her face lit up and she extended her hands for the bright blooms. With flushed cheeks, the man kissed her softly on the lips.

"'Tis sweet to see Mr. McNalley dote upon his sweetheart." Layla said, as she reached beneath her to grab more flower crowns for several little girls eagerly waving their money towards her. "They've been courting about thirty years or so now."

"Thirty years?" Baffled, Heidi looked to see if Layla was serious. The sister nodded.

"Aye. Both widowers tip-toeing around their former spouses' memories. But everyone knows they've loved one another a lifetime in itself."

"Why didn't they just get married?"

Layla shrugged. "No one knows. But every year, Mr. McNalley buys Anora a bundle of roses and kisses her publicly. The only time anyone sees them so bold."

"That is so sweet." Rhea walked up, hand on heart as she heard the rest of the story. "I couldn't imagine not wanting to marry Claron. I mean, I know he hasn't asked me yet, but now that I've found him I could not imagine going thirty years just flirting with him. I'd die."

Heidi and Layla snickered at her honesty.

"It's true." She pointed to Claron laughing across the way with Murphy and Jace. "I mean, look at the man. Have you ever seen a man so dreamy?"

"Ah, he's me brother, Rhea. I wouldn't exactly use the word 'dreamy,'" Layla replied, biting back a smile.

"And if you look at the men surrounding him, I'd say they all have their own 'dreamy' qualities about them," Heidi stated.

"Hmmm..." Rhea crossed her arms and studied the other O'Rifcan men. "I guess you're right. But Claron is the best."

"To you," Layla and Heidi said at the same time and rolled their eyes at Rhea's heavy sigh of pure delight.

"She's hopeless." Heidi shoved Rhea to force her to break her trance on Claron and get back to work.

"I am, and gladly so. I can't wait until the final flush so I can kiss him under the falling flowers." She squealed. "It's so romantic."

"Final flush?" Heidi asked.

"When the petals are released and the festival ends," Layla explained. "Followed by fireworks."

"Ah. I see."

"Most grab their love or sweetheart and plant a kiss on them to seal good luck for the coming year."

"It all comes down to luck for you Irishmen, doesn't it?"

"Aye," Layla agreed. "Keeping the fairies happy is one of our greatest and most serious tasks. Flower festival be a way to do that. And in return for showing off their beautiful flowers, the fairies see to it to that they keep us on their good side."

Rhea pointed. "There's Amelia Biden."

Layla snarled and had Rhea laughing. "Be nice."

Amelia, Claron's ex-girlfriend, walked up to the table. Warily, she made eye contact with Rhea and then Layla. Heidi stepped in front of the other two and offered a welcoming smile. "What can we get you?"

"Just one of the potted vases, please." Amelia handed Chloe money as Heidi reached behind her. "Here you go." Heidi handed her the small clay pot tied with a pink bow. Amelia eyed the necklaces around Layla, Chloe, and now Rhea's necks before turning and quietly making her way towards her own booth supporting her bookstore business. She set the pot on the corner of the table as part of her display. The O'Rifcan brothers stood near her table and not one acknowledged her presence, not even Claron, as they continued talking. *The poor woman*, Heidi thought. But her thought was interrupted as Jace branched away from his brothers and held a single rose out to Amelia. Hesitantly, the woman accepted it and a shy smile spread over her face at being thought of. Jace lingered a few moments speaking with her, and Heidi grinned. The O'Rifcan family made it their mission to make others feel special, and it melted her heart every time.

"My beautiful lasses," Murphy walked up, his arms outstretched. "If I had an entire field of flowers, it would not be enough to shower upon you all."

"What do you need, Murphy?" Chloe asked.

"Not a thing. I just wished to gaze upon beauty." He winked as he quickly snatched Heidi's hand and kissed the back of it. Murphy wore a flower crown, along with a necklace chain, a garland draped over his shoulders, blooms poking out of every pocket on his clothes, and a stem tucked behind each ear.

"You've been hard at work, I see." Heidi pointed to his appearance and he grinned wickedly.

"The beautiful women of Castlebrook just wish to make me feel special for a day."

"A day?" Rhea and Chloe asked doubtfully in unison.

Murphy laughed. "This be my favorite, though." He fingered a rose in his pocket. "Mam loves on us every year with her special touch. I expect all of you for a pint tonight." He tilted his head and waited for each woman to nod that they'd stop by the pub. "Good. Have a care, my little birds."

When Murphy left, Heidi sat in a chair and spent the rest of the afternoon helping hand out flowers to various hands as she laughed and talked with Rhea and the sisters. Overall, she ranked it as one of her most favorite experiences in Ireland. That and her date with Riley were experiences she would always remember. The sun began to set, and the soft light of dusk settled over the festival grounds. The live band set up outside of Murphy's began playing a lively tune that signaled the end of the festival was approaching. Rhea grabbed her hand and pulled her to her feet. "It's time for the grand finale." The four women linked arms and walked towards the middle of the street, meeting up with the rest of the O'Rifcan family. Sidna pulled each woman into a firm hug before settling next to Senior.

Claron stepped forward and gently took Rhea's hand and pulled her with him a few feet away, wrapping his arms around her waist as he rested his forehead against hers and softly spoke to her in Irish.

Riley walked up, and Heidi's heart fluttered a moment before disappointment settled in at the fact he stopped just short of her and stood next to one of his brothers. Chloe nudged her and nodded for her to head his direction. "'Tis the perfect time for boldness, Heidi love," She whispered.

"But I leave tomorrow," Heidi replied.

"Ah, but you have today," Chloe pointed out softly and nudged her forward towards Riley's back.

A pop sounded and a firework signal was sent into the air. It was not quite dark yet, so the firework show remained a few minutes away, but the signal was for the flowers to drop. As Heidi reached Riley's side, the windows to the surrounding buildings opened and flower petals were thrown. Blooms flooded the air, confetti raining down around them in thick clouds. Laughter, awe, and celebration sounded in the street. Claron pulled Rhea into a dip and kissed her soundly on the lips. Declan kissed his wife, Aine, as flowers fell around them. And Senior and Sidna... well, no one had to tell them twice. Roland, Rhea's Grandpa, stood near his granddaughter and laughed cheerfully at the sight of her and Claron. Heidi slid her hand in Riley's and he jolted a moment until he looked down and saw it was her. *Now or never*, she thought. And she stood to her tip toes and gently cupped his face with her free hand. Lightly, she pressed her lips to his. His body tensed, but instead of pulling away, his free hand slid to the back of her neck and as he slowly relaxed, he took the kiss deeper. Surprise hit her stomach and danced along her nerves, down to her toes, as he opened the floodgates of emotions she'd battled with for days. It was a dream. She floated on a soft sigh and flower petals as the sky deepened in color, the kiss deepened in severity, and her heart deepened in love for a man she'd tell goodbye.

∞

The crack and sizzle of fireworks broke Riley of his trance and pulled his lips away from Heidi's. Her eyes were full of unspoken words and a hint of regret as he studied her a moment, her chin in his hands. Her delicate face framed by his large palms, he brushed his thumbs over her cheeks. Regrettably, he released her face and squeezed her hand before kissing her palm. He needed air. Yes, he knew he was outside, but he needed a lung full and Heidi was stifling his airflow. He needed to step away from her before he poured out his heart and foolishly laid it at her feet. He stepped away, his hand slipping from hers. She stepped towards him, but he held up his hand. "This is where I leave you, Heidi love." He stuck his hands in his pockets so they would not betray him and reach for her again. "Safe travels to Texas." And as hard as it was, he turned and walked away.

It only took two steps before regret set in, but he stayed the course and headed straight for his truck that was parked behind Murphy's Pub. He'd miss the celebratory after party, and he was fine with that. Right now, he needed to separate himself from Heidi. He needed his own space, so his thoughts were set upon Limerick and his house. He'd brood, he knew, but he'd be productive. He'd work on Clary's house plans until too late an hour, sleep too late in the morning, so as to miss the time in which Heidi was to leave, and when he awakened, she'd be gone. Nothing he could do about it then. No quick trip to the airport for one last goodbye. Clean, efficient separation. It's what he needed. He couldn't look at her again, or he'd never let her leave. And that wasn't fair to her. It wasn't her fault he'd fallen for her. Then again, maybe it was her fault. He'd like to force the blame onto her, but the truth was he'd been lost the moment he laid eyes on her. As much as he scoffed at the idea, and at his parent's own love story, the fates thought it funny to pull the same trick on him. 'Twas a curse, really, that he should succumb to love in such a way. Was it not cruel to give such a heart as Heidi's to him and then strip her away?

Relieved, when he made it to his truck without social interaction, Riley cranked the engine and made the familiar drive towards home. Why couldn't he have found what Clary and Rhea had? Rhea had opted to stay in Ireland so easily. Her heart for Clary was strong and committed. She showed no fear for the future. She trusted everything to work out. Rhea was fearless, and so he thought, was Heidi, until recently. Heidi spoke a strong game. Appearing aloof in her flirtations, but there was heart there. A wounded heart as well. A stubborn heart. A heart scared to take a chance on him.

He could admit he wasn't the most stable of choices to fall in love with. Up until the last few weeks his own heart and mind were not even remotely interested in love or settling down. He enjoyed his dalliances. He enjoyed having his fun but then coming home to a quiet house.

He parked and walked the familiar footpath to his front door and unlocked it to step inside. As he hung his keys next to the entry, he absorbed the quiet. The memory of her draped over his leather sofa tattooed itself in his mind. Her winding up his staircase, long legs and teasing smile, etched in his memory. Going home was meant to make him feel better, instead, he felt lonely. On a growl, he made his way towards his office and pulled out the drafts for Clary's cottage. Perhaps helping his brother with his love project would help ease the hurt in his own chest.

He sat, running his hands through his hair, as his phone dinged. He glanced at the text. Rhea. She would be the one to text him to check up on him. The thought gave him a small smile. She'd sent him a picture of the fireworks.

Riley: *"Beautiful. Like you, Rhea darling. Happy First Flower Festival. Make Clary treat you to a celebratory pint."*

She didn't respond. And he was glad for it. He wasn't in the mood to appear fine. Though he knew Rhea would understand, it was the sympathy he couldn't handle at the moment. He also knew Rhea would miss Heidi as well. Misery deserved company, but not tonight. Perhaps they could miss Heidi together tomorrow, but tonight, Riley needed a break.

He leaned over his sketches, the design for Clary's cottage additions taking shape to be similar to his own house design. It was no secret Riley loved natural light and landscape. Clary's cottage sat atop a cliff overlooking Angel's Gap and the very idea of solid glass on the backside of the potential upstairs addition would offer a stunning view of the scenery. He'd have to convince Clary it was the way to go forward with the design, but it would not take much effort. If Clary thought it would impress Rhea, he'd do it. And Clary wanted to give Rhea a home as beautiful as she was. And Riley would help make his brother's dream happen.

At four minutes past three in the morning, Riley finally set his pencil down and spread out all of his new drafts. Clary's cottage had finally taken shape. Room for Rhea and their love. Room for potential little ones in the future. And private quarters for Roland, which was one of Clary's specific requests. Done. He shuffled the papers back into his portfolio, glancing at his watch in the process. How was it the wee hours of the morning and he still felt miserably awake? Convincing himself that a hot shower would ready him for sleep, he drifted up the stairs with heavy steps and heavy heart, praying God would grant him a night's rest and dreamless sleep.

«CHAPTER FOURTEEN»

"*Call me when you land.* No matter the time." Rhea hugged Heidi tightly, sniffling back tears as she reluctantly released her. "I'm so glad you came."

Heidi squeezed Rhea's hand once more before stepping into a warm embrace from Claron. "Take care of her, my sexy farmer."

He laughed and nodded. "'Tis my greatest pleasure to do so. You be careful, Heidi lass. Come see us again."

"Oh, that is a most definite yes." She hoisted her carry on over her shoulder. She soaked in one last look of the two. "You two are a fit. I like the look of you." Both flashed dazzling smiles. "Talk to you soon." She waved as she passed through airport security, noticing they did not walk away until she was out of sight. A weight settled upon her chest as she went through the motions of reading over her ticket to find her gate number. People bustled around her, rushing by, hurried to find their way to their next destination, but Heidi felt each step was agonizingly slow. She was in no hurry to leave. If she were to let her heart make the decision, she wouldn't be leaving, but she knew better than to let her heart lead the way. Wasn't that how she trapped herself in Baltimore for three years? She'd let her heart follow after Chase, and then she was too stubborn to leave. Too stubborn to admit she'd made the wrong move. So, she'd stayed and worked. Her time in Baltimore wasn't all miserable, it just wasn't home. Texas was home. Wasn't it? She walked to the windows overlooking the tarmac at Shannon International Airport and soaked in what little she could see of the Irish countryside beyond the bustle of planes and luggage carts.

She only had a thirty minute wait until her flight began boarding, and it was a good thing. She shouldered past the already seated passengers to find her seat in the middle on the left. Exit row. Pure bliss for her long legs. She lifted her carry on in the overhead bin and sat. She slipped her phone out and sent Rhea a text that she'd boarded and then began swiping through her photos. Picture after picture of her new friends flashed across her screen, and then she found it. The one picture she'd taken of Riley. It was while she was at his house beating him at pool that she'd snapped one of him. His sparkling blue eyes, dazzling teeth, and that hair that was to die for. She rubbed her finger over his face and then exited the album before she started crying. She was aggravated that he'd not called that morning or come to see her off at the B&B. Everyone else had come, but he'd stayed away. And that hurt. But could she blame him?

The kiss they'd shared the previous night at the festival still swam in her bones and made her heart flutter. He'd poured himself into her and then left her standing in the midst of a crowd. He hadn't even turned back to look at her one last time. Wasn't he supposed to do that? Isn't that how it was supposed to go? Wasn't he to show up to the airport at the last minute and beg her not to leave? Or somehow bypass security and evade the security guards as he rushed to find her gate? To find her? To confess his love for her and beg her to stay? No.

Life wasn't a movie, and if it were, Heidi knew her storyline would not involve such fluff. Rhea's maybe, but not hers. And that stung. Because that's what she wanted. She wanted Riley to come after her, and the fact that he hadn't disappointed her. A tear snuck through and landed on her hand and she quickly swiped it away so as to avoid prying eyes. She was not going to cry. She refused. She'd made her decision and she was going to stick to it. It was foolish to feel this way after only a couple of weeks. If she still felt this way in a few months, then maybe she'd consider making another trip. But right now, the best move was to head back to Texas, find a job, definitely move out of her parents' guest house, and start a new chapter. Determined, Heidi ignored the last remaining texts that began flooding her phone and stared out the window until take off.

∞

"Alright, here's a sample of my cream." Layla rubbed a lush cream over Riley's jaw as Rhea did the same to Claron. Murphy did his own, already complaining he did not have a pretty lass to do it for him. "Now, shave a bit. See how it feels compared to what you normally use."

"I hardly shave, Layla. I'm keeping me beard." Riley looked up at his sister and she fisted her hands on her hips.

"As am I," Claron stated.

"And me," Murphy grumbled.

"Then shave around it. Humor me, brothers." Layla waited as she watched them all hesitantly grab a razor and peer down into small mirrors sitting on the table. Each took hesitant strokes along their neckline to neatly shape around their scruff. "Well?"

All brothers quietly continued until reaching their stopping points. Claron walked over to the sink and rinsed his face, Rhea ready and waiting with a hand towel. Murphy followed, and Rhea took special care and tenderly blotted his face for him so as to boost his ego. He winked at her on his way back to the table. Riley followed suit and sat back in his chair. Claron rubbed a hand over the shaven areas. "'Tis smooth."

Murphy cupped his cheeks. "Like a wee baby's bottom."

"It will do." Riley grinned at his sister. "You have a knack, Layla, for making creams and potions."

"They're not potions." She heaved a tired sigh as Chloe walked into the room as if she were strutting the catwalk. She did a brief stop, and kicked out her leg, her now smooth leg, and then did a half turn and posed. "The cream for the legs is incredible." She beamed at her sister. 'Tis Rhea's turn to be guinea pig."

"Rhea," Rhea pointed at herself, "was a guinea pig before you all were. Apparently all my bath salts and lotions when I first arrived were from Layla's magic apothecary cabinet. And I've been a loyal customer... or beggar, ever since."

"Apothecary? As if I'm a wizard." Layla hooted with laughter.

"My skin and my hair feel like a dream, so I'd say you are." Rhea slipped an arm around the sister's waist and squeezed. "I'm proud of you."

"Oh posh." Layla waved away the praise, but her cheeks were stained a rosy pink.

"You should sell them," Rhea continued. "I know I sent several bottles home with Heidi because she loved them so much."

"I sent her with some too," Chloe added.

"And me," Layla said. All three women suddenly realized Heidi had hustled them so as to have a heavy stockpile and they laughed.

"She's a rustler from Texas," Murphy stated. "Seems she rounded up what she needed until her next visit."

Rhea's eyes briefly darted to Riley who sat silently, pretending to read the back of Layla's labels.

Sidna waltzed into the kitchen, her cheerful disposition glowing even more when she saw her children seated around the small table in the kitchen. "And what have we here? A beauty party?"

"Beauty?" All the men scoffed.

She made the rounds of kissing all on their cheeks. "You're me babes, therefore yes, you are all beautiful. And what smooth cheeks you all have."

"We are having a sample party, Mam." Chloe pointed to Layla. "Of Layla's concoctions."

"Needs to offer them for the masses, I've always said."

"Well, I will see what the next tourists think when they stay at Clary's cottage this weekend."

"Ah, you've convinced him to try once more?" Murphy's brows rose. "I've been at him for weeks."

"'Tis my beauty and charm that did it." Layla placed a hand on Claron's shoulder. "And the fact he'd be able to stay in close quarters to Rhea. I found him mighty agreeable after that."

Unashamed, Claron shrugged and reached up to clasp Rhea's hand as she stood next to him. "I'm a sucker for my Yank."

Sidna beamed. "As you should be. Any word from Heidi, Rhea? She settled in?"

"She is. She's temporarily living in her parents' guest house until she finds a job. But the hunt is on and she seems hopeful."

"Ah, good. Miss her presence around here. She was my early bird. Chat over our tea and coffees.

Though I don't miss having to make an extra loaf of bread in the mornings." She chuckled at the memory. "Next you speak to her, you tell her my hellos."

"I will." Rhea cast a quick glance at Riley again, she and Sidna exchanging worried looks.

"And what of you, lad?" Sidna rubbed a hand down his hair. "You in Galway this week?"

"Aye." He pushed back from the table and stood. "Until me work there is done."

"Coming along?" Rhea asked.

"It is. It be a beast, but I've had worse projects."

"You look tired, boyo." Sidna cupped his face and tilted it from one side to the other. "But your skin feels lovely." She smiled at Layla as Riley crossed his eyes. Sidna patted his cheek and released him. "All I ask, Riley love, is that you make an appearance once a week for the meal, so I can cluck over you."

"How could I resist that?" Riley hugged his mam and picked up the shaving cream. "I'll be taking this one, Layla."

"And will you be paying for it then?" she countered.

He reached into his back pocket and retrieved his wallet, tossing money onto the table. "Will that be enough?"

Her eyes widened at the exorbitant amount and nodded. "That be plenty."

"Bang on then." He offered a departing wave to everyone else as he slipped out the back door. He'd take a walk along the river, as was his custom when he visited his parents, and perhaps his mood would lift.

He spotted Roland and his da casting their lines into the water. Much like Rhea, Roland's finesse with the fly rod spoke of years of practice. His father, a decent match, still did not have the smooth release like Roland. He waved to them.

"Riley, boyo." Senior beamed and his voice beckoned his son to come towards them. "Grab a rod, sit a spell, and help us catch some sup."

"I can't stay too long, Da. Need to be home to pack a bag for work next week."

"Humor me." Senior's voice was stern enough that Riley complied by sitting on the bank and baiting a line on a rod and reel. "You smell a bit fancy there."

"Layla's creams."

"Might need to try some myself," Roland added. "Rhea speaks highly of them."

Riley looked up at the two older men, both studying him. He set his rod down and leaned back on his hands, legs splayed out in front of him. "The two of you have something to say to me, best be on with it. I know you did not call me over to talk of Layla's creams."

The men exchanged a look.

"'Tis about Heidi, boyo," Senior started.

Riley held up his hand. "I don't wish to talk of Heidi, Da."

"Riley," Roland began. "It's evident you care for the girl."

"And what good does that do?" Riley barked and then inhaled a deep breath to calm his temper. "I'm sorry Roland. Da. Just... tired."

"No, you're in love, boyo." Senior laughed at his own statement. "Twists a man up, it does."

Riley picked a blade of grass and rubbed it between his fingers before tossing it to the ground. "It's miserable."

The older men laughed and nodded.

"Only miserable because you let her leave," Senior pointed out.

"Let her? Like I could have stopped her," Riley countered. "Heidi's a strong mind and a will to match. There be no stopping her."

"Did you tell her how you felt?" Roland asked.

"No. Why would I? I'd only known her a couple weeks. I did not want her to think me a loon."

"Whoa there, lad," Senior warned. "Your Mammy didn't think I was crazy for wanting to marry her after a week."

"I'm not ready to marry Heidi," Riley admitted. "I just wanted more time with her."

"And so you make time," Senior continued.

"How? My work is hectic. I'm in the beginning stages of a large building project. She's starting a new life in Texas. The time is wrong. I met her at the wrong time in both our lives. Perhaps if I'd met her a few years ago, or two years from now it could have worked, but now... it just can't. For both of us."

"Seems to me you are speaking a lot for her," Roland pointed out. "I bet she'd hate that. Being a strong mind and all."

"She would, no doubt," Senior agreed. "Have you spoken to the lass since she left?"

"No."

Surprised, Senior eyed his son. "And why not?"

"Because it is best to move along. If I speak to her it would only make me feel worse."

"And why is that?"

"Because I know she does not feel the same, Da." Riley tossed a stone into the water and watched as the river lapped it up. "Heidi wanted my attention, not my heart. It was my foolish decision to give her both."

"Foolish, yes." Senior handed his rod to Roland and eased down next to his son. "But it takes a bit of foolishness to chase after love. It's a risk. A risk only fools take. But if you two should work out, imagine the happiness you will have. No more feeling blue."

"I can't ask her to move here, not after her life in Baltimore. Would not be fair."

"Then you go to her."

Riley shook his head. "Everything I've worked for is here. I've built my business. I'm in the middle of one project, about to start a second. I can't just leave."

"Then perhaps it is not love after all, and you are right to ignore your feelings for the lass. If you loved her, you'd be willing to give anything for her." He slapped a comforting hand on Riley's shoulder and stood, accepting his rod from Roland. "Now, be on with ye, boyo, before your brooding scares the fish away."

Harrumphing, Riley stood to his feet. "Be seeing you."

The two older men waved and then began predicting Riley's next moves as if they could call the shots.

∞

"I hope you have a giant glass of wine." Heidi plopped her purse on the counter top as her mother turned from the refrigerator.

"Hey honey. Nothing today?" Sarah Rustler slid a stemmed glass towards her daughter and eased onto a vacant stool as Heidi did the same.

"Nothing. The interview was ridiculous today. I have no idea why JoAnne thought I'd be interested in that place."

"She's just trying to help you get on your feet, baby."

"Ugh, I know." Heidi rubbed her hands through her hair and fluffed it in frustration. "I need to call Rhea. And vent."

"Will be late there, honey. You might want to wait until in the morning."

Heidi calculated the time difference on her fingers and sighed. "Maybe she'll be up. She's still living in Limerick, so I imagine she's not asleep yet. City never sleeps, as they say. I'm going to give it a try. I need to see how everyone is doing. Hear some cheerful news."

"What about Riley?"

"What about him?" Heidi's eyes were sharp.

"You could call him," her mother suggested.

"And why would I do that?"

Sighing, Sarah stood and walked towards the stove and lightly stirred the vegetables in the skillet. "It's obvious you care for the boy. You haven't been the same since you came home. You won't speak of him. When before, all your emails were about him."

"He hasn't reached out to me either," Heidi pointed out. "So obviously he does not miss me."

"Or he could be just as miserable as you. How will you know unless you phone him and talk to him?"

"I'm not brave enough for that yet," Heidi admitted. "I'll call Rhea first."

"Heidi Rustler... afraid?" Sarah shook her head. "I'm surprised at you, sweetie."

Heidi grabbed her glass and trudged out the patio doors and plopped into a wooden chair. She dialed Rhea's number and waited. Hopefully Rhea answered. She needed to hear her voice. Needed to hear more about the people she'd left behind. She missed them. And she missed Riley, no matter what she said to her mother.

"Heidi?" Rhea's sleepy voice flooded over the line. "It's late. Or early. It's... I was sleeping," Rhea mumbled.

"Well wake up. I need to talk."

"Give me a sec."

She heard rustling over the phone and then heard the soft sounds of glasses tinkering against one another. Rhea would be making tea, she realized, settling in for a long chat. Heidi loved her for that. She'd be too nice to say no to a late-night phone call.

"You in Castlebrook?"

"No. Limerick. Heavy workload this week, so I'm staying here until Friday. Now tell me what's up? How'd the interview go today?"

"Terrible." Heidi explained the overly positive receptionist and the chipper office manager.

"You're right. They sound awful. Happy employers are the worst," Rhea jested. "So what's the real problem?"

Sighing, Heidi propped her feet on a stool. "I'm not sure if I made the right decision."

"Leaving Ireland?" Hope resounded in Rhea's voice.

"No. Leaving Baltimore. I had a great job there. A bit boring at times, but at least I had a steady job. I'm having a hard time here, Rhea."

"What if I could get you a job here in Limerick, would you come back here?"

"No."

"Why not?"

"Because I'm meant to be here."

"You were just questioning your move to Texas!" Rhea's exasperation rang through the phone. "What is going on with you? And be honest."

Heidi thumbed the hem of her blouse, a loose string distracting her for a moment.

"Heidi?" Rhea asked again.

"I miss him." There. She'd said it. She'd finally admitted to missing Riley. And surprisingly, she felt relief instead of shame.

Rhea fell quiet a moment. "Have you spoken to him?" she asked.

"No."

"You could call him."

"You sound like my mother," Heidi grumbled.

"It's been a few weeks, Heidi. If you miss him, call him up. I guarantee you he will be glad to hear from you."

"Oh, you guarantee that?"

Rhea's brief hesitation had Heidi palming her face in her hand. "I think it would be a nice surprise." Rhea continued. "Because he's missed you too."

"Yeah?"

"Yes." Rhea smiled faintly into the phone. Though Riley had not told her of his feelings, she could read the man like a book. "He's been about as miserable as you sound."

"I don't want to just hear his voice." Heidi bit her thumb nail as her mind whirled with new ideas of traveling back to Ireland. Was she crazy to think she could make a life over there? Rhea had succeeded in doing so. Why couldn't she? Would Riley even want to see her? "It would be insane."

"It's just a phone call," Rhea stated.

"No. Not that. Moving there. It would be crazy."

"Why? I did it. And it's been the smartest idea I've ever had."

"But you're in love with Clary. Of course it makes sense for you."

"And by the sounds of it, you're in love with Riley. So I don't see the problem here, Heidi."

"Ummm... he doesn't know I love him. And I have no idea if he feels the same."

"Listen, at some point you're just going to have to take a chance. You can either call him and gauge his feelings that way, or you can come back and surprise him, and share your heart then. Either way, it's a risk. But you are the one that has to live with the consequences of doing either one of those or nothing at all."

"But what if it turns out like Baltimore?"

"Then you will spend a few years with your best friend in a beautiful country. Aunt Grace seems to have enjoyed the single life all these years in Galway, who's to say you couldn't too?" Rhea laughed at her own statement, the thought of her flirtatious aunt making both women smile.

Sighing, Heidi sat a moment weighing Rhea's words in her heart. It was a risk. But could she live with herself if she never attempted the move? "Rhea," Heidi scooted to the edge of her seat in determination. "I'm going to need your help."

"Atta girl. I was hoping you would say that." Rhea chuckled into the phone. "Tell me what you're planning."

∞

"Clary, you're just going to have to trust me on this, alright? I know it's a bit of a change, but I believe it will capture your spot on the cliffs perfectly." Riley waited until his younger brother nodded and he pulled out his stack of sketches. "Okay, so here's me thought."

"Is that an upstairs?" Claron interjected.

"Yes, if you'll just wait to see wh—"

"Is that glass?"

"Clary, let me do the showing."

"How do you expect me to—"

"Clary!" Riley slapped a hand on the table and Claron fell silent. "Good. Now listen. I will explain the plans to you and then you can ask your questions and give your thoughts. Deal?"

Claron waved his hand. "I'm listening."

"Alright. I know you're attached to the cottage the way it is, but to be honest if you plan to romance Rhea enough to marry you one day, you're going to need more space for all the little ones you will more than likely be popping out. So—"

Claron choked on a laugh as nerves hit him full force and he reached for his beer.

"Have I lost you already?" Riley teased.

"A bit early to be talkin' of babes," Claron explained.

"But 'tis necessary when talking in terms of house and home."

"Aye, I guess you're right. All assuming I can convince Rhea to live at the cottage."

"And you will. Once you've asked her to marry you."

"Which I haven't even planned yet, brother. When I asked you to make changes to me house, I was honestly expecting a new kitchen and living space. Not an entirely new house."

"But why just a new kitchen when you could really jazz up the place and keep its original charm?" Riley tapped his pencil on the sketches. "Now, see how I've only drafted the second story over the back half of the cottage? This will make the front appear to be the same, but the back portion is the addition. An expanded living space with the second story on top of that, where the new master bedroom and bath will be, and a lovely sitting area that overlooks the Gap. You know Rhea loves the Gap, and what better view to give her. A giant romantic gesture, brother." Pleased with himself, Riley watched as Claron's green eyes perused the papers.

"And what of Roland?"

"Ah, yes." Riley shifted papers. "Roland be here." He pointed to Claron's current master bedroom. "'Tis toward the back of the house currently, so he'd have his privacy. We'd add a bit more here, extending the patio out so as to give him a small living space inside the room, but for the most part the rest remains the same. The other bedrooms be staying the same."

"You think Roland would want to be down the hall from little ones?"

"Ah, so now we're talking of little ones?" Riley teased.

"Just... processing," Claron admitted.

"I don't think Roland would care one bit. He'd be pleased to be a part of it all. Should you actually convince him to give up his flat."

"He needs to." Claron was resolute. "Not good for him going up and down those steps so much, with his cane and all. No matter what he says."

"Then there you have it. He'll be agreeable. Rhea will say yes to marrying you, you will have a dozen babies together, and all of me hard work won't be in vain." Riley leaned back and took a swig of his own beer. "So when do you plan on asking her?"

"When I've a mind to," Claron said, eyeing his brother. "I'm in no rush. Neither is Rhea. Seems everyone else wishes to rush us into matrimony, and obviously babes."

Riley laughed. "Only because we do not want you being stupid and ruining things. Rhea's a keeper. Just trying to secure her for you, brother."

"Aye. Everyone seems attentive to that task."

They both laughed at that.

"Speaking of lasses," Claron continued. "You speak to Heidi lately?"

"No. Not since the festival."

Claron's brows rose. "Really? That surprises me."

"Why? She left."

"Yikes." Claron took a long pull on his beer. "That sounded a bit bitter, brother."

"Perhaps I am. A bit," Riley admitted. "But Heidi is not the point of our conversation. You and Rhea are. Now let's get back to the drawings."

"No." Claron eased to his feet and stretched his back. "I like your plans, Riley. Though I'm not a fan of drastic change, you're right in the regard of expanding for me future. Though it terrifies me to think of, I need to plan for it all. I'm settled on these plans."

"Alright then. I'll just throw me pitch in the bin then. I thought it would take me longer to convince you."

"I wish to spoil my love." Claron shrugged as if he couldn't help it. "Your plans will do that. And it will mean much to Rhea knowing you designed it with her in mind."

"I do have a soft spot for your lass, Clary. Always have. Probably always will."

"And she for you." Claron smirked. "Though she likes me best."

Riley laughed. "As she should, because the two of you fit like puzzle pieces. It's really quite sickening."

Claron grinned. "Says you. Though I know you've been a bit blue, brother, over Heidi leaving." Claron held up his hand so Riley would let him finish. "But I think it's been good for you. You've never found a woman to twist you up so much. I think it will be good for you in the long run. Settle you more. Tame down your flirtations."

Riley chuckled. "Oh come now, Clary. I can't give up all my flirting. Then I just wouldn't be who I am."

"That's the truth of it too. But perhaps you can hand some of it off to Murphy."

"As if he needs more," Riley pointed out.

"That be the truth too." Claron laughed. "Anyway... I'm here if ye need to talk of her. I can't imagine if Rhea had decided to go back to Maryland what I would have done. She'd already won me over so. What I'm trying to say is that I'm here for ye, brother. Long as you need."

"Thanks, Clary. I'll be fine as long as I stay busy."

Claron's phone rang and Rhea's name popped up on the screen.

"Ah, speaking of your happily ever after." Riley grinned as Claron swiped the screen and lifted the phone to his ear.

"And how you know when I'm talking about you, I will never know," Claron laughed into the phone, his entire aura brightening as he spoke to his love.

His face paled a moment. "Now? Are you certain? Aye. I'm with him now. Are you sure about this?"

Claron stood and walked his beer to the sink and poured it out, tossing the bottle into the bin. Riley watched him curiously. "Rhea love," he continued. "I'm not sure of this... And she was agreeable to this?" A pause. "Chloe and Layla are there to help you. And Conor? I see..." He waited a breath. "Very well then. I'll bring Riley. What time you wish for us there? Bang on then, love. See you then." He hung up.

"It would seem that my darling Rhea is throwing a house party. At me cottage. Currently without me. We are to head there now."

Riley laughed. "See, she already feels so at home that she takes over your house."

"Aye, well, apparently everyone wishes to use my cottage for their own devices. First Layla and Murphy, now Rhea. We shall see how her first party goes." Claron eyed Riley's back with worry as Riley turned to toss his empty bottle into the trash. He especially wondered how his brother would react to one particular guest.

«CHAPTER FIFTEEN»

"A little to the left, Conor," Layla ordered, as their friend pulled the banner a tad higher. "Perfect. Pin it there." Conor pushed a thumb tack into the beam and slowly made his way down the ladder.

"Adds a nice bit of color, doesn't it?" Conor acknowledged Layla's handy work and she nodded.

"'Twas the point. Clary's house has always needed more color."

"Perhaps when he exchanges the nuptials with Rhea she could bring a pop or two with her."

"That'd be the day," Layla stated. "Rhea's house is just as neutral as Clary's. 'Tis quite a shame really, not having me as their decorator."

"A little help!" Chloe called as she attempted to open the cottage back door with her foot while balancing three large sacks in her arms. Conor hurried forward and scooped up her entire load and set them on the kitchen counter. "Thank you, Conor. Murphy's behind me with the drinks."

Conor nodded and hurried out the door towards Murphy's truck to lend a hand.

"Any word?" Layla asked.

"Clary is to bring Riley in a half hour. Rhea will arrive with the guest of honor not five minutes after. I'm to text her when Riley is here." Chloe swiped a hand over her forehead and looked at the decorations Layla had distributed throughout the house. "How do you feel about Heidi's return?"

Layla slid to a seat on one of the stools and began pulling contents out of the grocery bags. "I'm surprised, really. Figured she was too strong a head to come back on her own. I thought it would take Riley flying to Texas to convince her."

"Aye, I thought so too."

"But this is better. Heidi needed to be the one to make the decision. Now, Riley can decide what to do about it."

"You think he loves her?" Chloe retrieved a pound of butter and immediately slid it down the counter towards the mixer that stood there, so as to remind herself to make a dessert.

"I do. He won't admit it, the fool. But in his way, I think Riley's been snagged by the love bug. Will it be enough for the two of them to make something work? Who knows?"

"Rhea keeps saying Heidi is only coming to work and live here to see if she likes it, not that she's coming back for Riley. You think that's true?"

"Posh." Layla shook her head. "Heidi can say what she wants, but her heart is as much Riley's as his is hers."

Chloe's smile softened. "Odd. Our brothers finding lasses so quickly. Seeing Clary turn to mush has been amusing. Seeing Riley so serious and quiet... as if he be stunned."

"If it's a spell, I hope it's catching," Layla admitted. "I could use a good love spell."

"That so?" Chloe grinned in surprise. "You still longing for Gage?"

"Oh no," Layla replied. "He was just a dabble."

"Perhaps, once you've settled a bit in your new plans of business, love will find you."

"Perhaps so. Speaking of business, 'tis still okay to share your shop?"

"Of course." Chloe beamed. "I enlisted Conor to help transform the space. He has a gift with crafting."

"That he does. Thank you, sister."

The door opened, and Murphy and Conor bustled inside, arms burdened by beer crates.

"Tubs with ice are on the patio, Murphy. Drinks be set in the cold there," Chloe ordered.

"Yes ma'am, little one." Murphy tugged one of Chloe's bright red curls.

A horn honked, and several cars pulled in around the cottage and parked. Sidna, Senior, and Roland emerged from one, while the other O'Rifcan siblings spilled out of the others. Little Rose hopped out of Lorena's car and darted towards the cottage in search of Clary, pure disappointment settling over her features when she saw he wasn't there. A bark sounded and Rugby, Claron's Irish Setter, bounded from the dairy barn with lolling tongue and wagging tail towards the small girl, his happy licks of pure delight making her giggle. Holstein, Claron's cat, weaved his way through Sidna's legs until she scooped him up and carried him like a baby, stroking his head and sending him into content purrs as she bustled into the cottage.

"Seems the cavalry has arrived." Conor laughed. "I be on my way now, Chloe. Unless you need me for anything else."

"You aren't staying?" she asked, she and Layla both pinning him with a curious stare.

"Ah, I believed this to be a family gathering."

"Aye," Chloe admitted. "But you be family Conor. Best of friends and all."

Layla watched as Conor's eyes softened towards her sister's comment.

"If you're sure."

"We are," both sisters said.

He nodded, a tinge of pink coloring his ruddy cheeks. "That be the way of it then. I'll go help Murphy load the drinks. Make meself useful." Slightly embarrassed, Conor slipped outside.

"Bless him," Sidna said, watching Conor reteat as she settled Holstein on a chair and made her way into Claron's kitchen. "And what be the plan for food?"

Layla and Chloe pointed towards the refrigerator and Sidna opened the door, clicking her tongue. "Not near enough. Let me make a call."

Chloe and Layla rolled their eyes at one another as they heard their mother on the phone with Mrs. McCarthy.

Layla glanced at her watch. "'Tis time for Riley's arrival. And on time they are." She looked out the window as Claron and Riley walked up to the house, Claron topping to scoop up Rose on his way and settling her on his shoulders. They both ducked inside.

"Why the party at Clary's?" Riley asked.

"Rhea's idea. She wanted us all in one place."

"And she couldn't do that at Mam's for the meal?"

"Enjoy, brother. Our Rhea wishes to host a party. Her first one," Chloe pointed out. "We best make it grand for her."

"Please do," Claron said, as he eyed all of the colorful decorations around his house.

"Only temporary," Layla murmured and had him chuckling.

"And where is our darling Rhea?" Riley asked. "Late to her own party?"

"She had an errand," Layla stated, as she nudged Chloe out the door so as to escape further questioning.

"Something feels off." Riley looked to Claron and his brother shrugged.

"Alright, keep your secrets, brother. But if Rhea proposes to you today, I would not be surprised."

"She not be after a proposal today," Claron replied. "She has something else up her sleeve."

"Not sure I like your Rhea being mischievous," Riley teased. "Doesn't settle well."

Claron laughed. "Aye. A new side to her, that is for certain."

"Boys," Sidna interrupted. "Clary put Rose down on the floor. You two need to be arranging chairs around the tables outside. And when Conor's mammy arrives, help her unload the food. Honestly, me girls throwing a party with hardly any food." She tisked her tongue as she grabbed the pound of butter Chloe had left on the counter and immediately set about the kitchen pulling ingredients from Claron's cupboards.

Mumbled agreements of obedience to their mother's wishes had the two brothers stepping outside as Rhea's small compact car rolled up to the house. Layla called inside the house for her mother to come outside. The show was about to start, and she grinned when her eyes settled on her unassuming older brother.

∞

Heidi nervously wound her hands in her lap as Rhea pulled to a stop and people mingled around Claron's yard and cottage. Her heart pounded when she spotted Riley's dark hair amongst them, his attention on helping Murphy and Conor shift crates.

"Does he know I'm coming?" She turned to Rhea, who looked equally nervous. Not reassuring in the slightest.

"No." Sighing, Rhea reached for her hand and squeezed. "It's going to be great. Totally fine."

Heidi muffled a disbelieving laugh. "You're a terrible liar, Rhea. Always have been. Besides, are you trying to encourage me or yourself?"

"Both. So, I'll try a new tactic. I don't know if it will be an incredible reunion. *But*," she stressed. "I believe it will be because I know how much he cares for you and how much you care for him."

"And if it isn't?"

"You're moving here to start a new chapter, much like me. Whether Riley chooses to be a part of it does not weigh into your overall decision. He's more of a... bonus, so to speak."

"He would hate you for saying that." Heidi chuckled as she saw Chloe wave their direction.

Rhea leaned over and hugged Heidi tightly. "I'm proud of you for coming. And excited to have you living here, no matter how long." A sniffle had Heidi pulling back and groaning.

"Don't you start that, Rhea." Heidi's own voice broke as she lightly dabbed her own eyes with a tissue.

"I'm sorry, I'm just so happy you're here. And I can't wait for Riley to see you. I'm so nervous for you, but happy and proud. Too many emotions for one girl to handle."

"Then let's get out of this car and see what happens, because it's starting to kill me not knowing."

"Alright. Here we go." Rhea reached for her door handle.

"Wait!" Heidi frantically called, Rhea turning towards her friend and receiving a blow of air in the face. "How's my breath?"

Rhea burst into a laugh and shook her head. "It's fine. Come on." She stepped out as Heidi was mumbling that she had to be ready just in case things went her way.

They walked up the hill and Claron met them half way, kissing each on the cheek. "Good to see you, Heidi. It's been a while."

"Only a few weeks, Claron, but good to hear my handsome farmer hasn't forgotten me. You're looking especially cheery today." She enfolded him in a friendly hug, always comforted by his laid-back presence.

"Pleased with my lass, throwing her first party." He squeezed Rhea around the waist.

"At your house," Rhea pointed out.

Claron shrugged. "I'm glad you thought of it. 'Tis important to me that you wished to have it here."

"Alright cuties," Heidi nudged them aside. "Stop with the love stuff."

"She's nervous," Rhea told Claron, not trying to keep her voice down.

"Ah." Claron pointed towards the farthest round table where Riley sat with Conor and Lorena's husband, Paul. Deep in conversation, he did not see Heidi approaching or hear the deafening silence that fell upon the rest of his family as they spotted her. It wasn't until Conor went to sip his beer and choked a moment at the sight of her behind his friend, that had Riley turning on a laugh. His laugh fell silent in a heartbeat as Heidi stood about five feet from him. He eased to his feet as he noticed the remainder of his family watching and waiting.

"Hi there, Riley," Heidi greeted with a nervous wave. She watched as the blue of his eyes sparked, and a firm scowl crossed his face. He crossed his arms.

"Heidi. What brings you back to Ireland?"

Her chin quivered a moment, her nerves betraying her as she saw the hurt in his expression. His shoulders relaxed a moment when she felt the first tear slide down her cheek.

Uncrossing his arms, he stepped towards her, sliding his palm to cup her cheek. His thumb swiping away her tear. His touch was gentle as his eyes searched hers. "What brings you back, Heidi?" he asked again.

She felt her pulse quicken as he held her gaze, and her heart and mind sounded in agreement as she closed the space between them and placed her lips to his. Slowly, he responded, and then eagerly, cheers erupting around them. He swept her off her feet and spun her around, a cheerful squeal escaping her lips and making him laugh.

Celebration vibrated through her as she heard the O'Rifcan family and those closest to them cheering for her and Riley's reunion. He set her to her feet and pressed his forehead to hers, sliding his hands down her arms to link his fingers with hers. "About time you came to your senses, love. I was losing patience."

She bit her tongue as she just rolled her eyes at him and the pure glee shining on his face. "You're going to be trouble, Riley O'Rifcan, I already know it."

"And yet you're here," he added, pulling her to him in a tight embrace.

"Yes. I'm here."

"For good?"

"For as long as you'll have me," she admitted nervously.

He pulled back to look into her face. "Then for good it is." Kissing, they ignored his mam's call to feast, but could not dodge the exuberant hug from Rhea as she pounced on them in excitement. "Welcome home, Heidi." She squeezed them both tightly before Claron gently tugged her away.

"You've changed my life, Heidi Rustler." Riley tenderly slid her hair over her shoulder and smoothed his hand down the back of it. "I hoped you would take the risk and come back."

"Why didn't you just tell me that?"

"You needed to figure it out on your own."

"And what if I didn't? Would you have come for me?"

His lips quirked as he reached into his back pocket and slipped out his cell phone and swiped towards his latest internet search. Plane tickets to Texas appeared on his screen and a happy sob escaped her lips before she wrapped her arms around his neck and held him close.

"Like I said, I was losing patience. You have a way about you, Heidi love. I was not about to let you slip through me fingers. Now," He linked her arm with his and turned her towards the party. "It would seem our Rhea wishes to celebrate your homecoming. As do I."

Continue the story with...

Book Three of
The Siblings O'Rifcan Series

**All Books in
The Siblings O'Rifcan Series:**
Claron
Riley
Layla
Chloe
Murphy

**All titles by Katharine E. Hamilton
Available on Amazon and Amazon Kindle**

Adult Fiction:

The Unfading Lands Series
The Unfading Lands, Part One
Darkness Divided, Part Two
Redemption Rising, Part Three

The Lighthearted Collection
Chicago's Best
Montgomery House
Beautiful Fury

Children's Literature:
The Adventurous Life of Laura Bell
Susie At Your Service
Sissy and Kat

Short Stories:
If the Shoe Fits

Find out more about Katharine and her works at:

www.katharinehamilton.com

Social Media is a great way to connect with Katharine. Check her out on the following:

Facebook: Katharine E. Hamilton
https://www.facebook.com/Katharine-E-Hamilton-282475125097433/

Twitter: @AuthorKatharine
Instagram: @AuthorKatharine

Contact Katharine:
khamiltonauthor@gmail.com

ABOUT THE AUTHOR

Katharine E. Hamilton began writing a decade ago by introducing children to three fun stories based on family and friends in her own life. Though she enjoyed writing for children, Katharine moved into adult fiction in 2015 with the release of her first novel, The Unfading Lands, a clean, epic fantasy that landed in Amazon's Hot 100 New Releases on its fourth day of publication and reached #72 in the Top 100 Bestsellers on all of Amazon in its first week. The series did not stop there and the following two books in The Unfading Lands series released in late 2015 and early 2016.

Though comfortable in the fantasy genre, Katharine decided to venture into romance in 2017 and released the first novel in a collection of sweet, clean romances: The Lighthearted Collection. The collection's works would go on to reach bestseller statuses and win Reader's Choice Awards and various Indie Book Awards in 2017 and early 2018.

Katharine has contributed to charitable Indie anthologies and helped other aspiring writers journey their way through the publication process. She loves everything to do with writing and loves that she can continue to share heartwarming stories to a wide array of readers.

She was born and raised in the state of Texas, where she currently resides on a ranch in the heart of brush country with her husband, Brad, and their son, Everett, and their two furry friends, Tulip and Cash. She is a graduate of Texas A&M University, where she received a Bachelor's degree in History.

She is thankful to her readers for allowing her the privilege to turn her dreams into a new adventure for us all.